TO LOVE AGAIN

Jenny Doyle had always loved her brother-in-law, Jake Thomas-Harding, but when he chose to marry her sister instead, she knew it was a love that had no future. Now his wife is dead, and he asks Jenny to live under his roof to look after his little daughter. She wonders what the future holds for them all, especially when ghosts of the past arise to haunt them . . .

CATRIONA McCUAIG

TO LOVE AGAIN

Complete and Unabridged

LINFORD
Leicester

First published in Great Britain in 2002

First Linford Edition
published 2008

British Library CIP Data

McCuaig, Catriona
   To love again.—Large print ed.—
Linford romance library
1. Love stories
2. Large type books
I. Title
823.9′2 [F]

ISBN 978–1–84782–072–3

Published by
F. A. Thorpe (Publishing)
Anstey, Leicestershire

Set by Words & Graphics Ltd.
Anstey, Leicestershire
Printed and bound in Great Britain by
T. J. International Ltd., Padstow, Cornwall

1

Jenny came to herself with a start when she almost bumped into the untidy young man, who now stood glaring at her as he juggled the carrier bags he was carrying in an effort to keep them from falling.

'Hey, look where you're going!' he exclaimed.

'Sorry,' she muttered, edging past him.

'I should jolly well think so!'

His words drifted back to her as she hurried on, but she didn't care. She had better things to think about than the snappish cries of a spotty-faced youth. She had a problem, a real dilemma, and she couldn't decide what to do about it. At least, she admitted to herself, she did know, deep down, what she meant to do. It was just that everyone else told her it was madness to go and keep house for her widowed brother-in-law. Was it possible that they were right?

Gran had been shocked.

'Jane Elizabeth Doyle! You can't mean it, going to live with Jake Thomas-Harding?'

'I'm not going to live with him, Gran. It's not like that. He just wants me to look after little Sheena.'

'People will talk.'

'Oh, Gran!'

Her grandmother frowned.

'This may be the Fifties, but don't you 'oh, Gran' me, my girl. Nothing much has changed since my young day. You'll ruin your reputation and no decent man will want to marry you.'

Jenny bit back the hot words which sprang to mind, and said mildly, 'I'll be well chaperoned, Gran, with the cook and the housekeeper there.'

'That's a matter of opinion, but I've no doubt you'll go your own road in the end, no matter what I say. Mark my words, this will end in tears, and don't say I didn't warn you!'

The older woman was genuinely concerned, but having said her piece she was determined to go no further. After a life full of ups and downs she had adopted a fatalistic attitude. Like everyone else, the girl must make her own mistakes, and live with the consequences.

Jenny fared no better with Doris, her stepmother.

'I don't know what your father will have to say about this, I'm sure!'

'Dad won't care.'

Jenny's father had retreated into his shell after his beloved younger daughter had been killed in a car crash, and now he divided his time between work and his allotment, communicating with his wife and remaining daughter as little as possible.

'Hmph! I hope Jake pays you well, that's all I can say. I suppose you'll have to give up your job at Benson's, and I can't manage without your money coming in, little as it is. I hope he's thought about that!'

Jenny had no intention of paying for her keep when she was no longer living in the house, but she knew better than to say anything along those lines. Her stepmother made no secret of the fact that she barely tolerated her presence in the home, now that her own daughter was gone. Soon after Ruth's death, Jenny had overheard Doris Doyle speaking to a friend.

'Why did my Ruth have to die, Phyllis? Why was she taken, while that Jenny is still here? Why couldn't it have been the other way around?'

Desperately hurt, Jenny told herself that these were the words of a grieving mother, but they continued to rankle nevertheless. It was horrid to think that somebody wished she had died in her sister's place.

Jenny couldn't remember her own mother, Elizabeth, who had died young. All that remained was a faded snap of a young woman holding the baby who had been her own little Jenny. But Elizabeth had never been strong and had died giving birth to a little boy, Frank, a longed-for son. The baby had survived his mother by just a few hours. Left with a two-year-old daughter to care for, Jenny's father had soon remarried and in due course fathered another little girl, Ruth.

Ruth was the kind of toddler everyone cooed over. With her blonde curls and big blue eyes, her bewitching smiles and infectious giggles, she completely overshadowed shy, dark-haired Jenny. She sailed through adolescence, bypassing the usual gawky stage, and grew into a beautiful, young woman, adored by every boy she met. As if that wasn't enough she was clever at school, as Gran put it.

'I'm waiting!'

Doris's sharp tones cut through Jenny's daydream.

'I want to know what you plan to do! And it's ridiculous if Jake expects you to give up working at Benson's. Good jobs don't grow on every tree!'

Jenny shrugged.

'I don't know, Mum. Nothing's been decided yet.'

'I know what's on your mind, my girl! It's the thought of living in that fine house, with servants to cook and clean for you. You always were jealous of poor Ruth. Now you want to step into her shoes. Oh, you can pull a face,' she went on, seeing Jenny's anguished expression. 'I saw the way you looked at their wedding, as if you'd lost a pound and found sixpence. Couldn't bear the thought of your sister falling on her feet, could you?'

The words stung. Doris had come too near to the truth, but nobody would ever know the pain Jenny had felt that day, dressed in pink taffeta in her rôle of bridesmaid, watching her sister being married to Jake Thomas-Harding, the man they both loved.

'Someone has to look after little Sheena,' she replied, managing to swallow the lump that came into her throat as she tried to push away the memory.

'Let him hire a nanny, then. He can afford it.'

'Sheena has retreated into her shell since her mother died. The doctor says it's shock. After all, she was in the car when the accident happened. She may be too young to really understand what happened, but it's bound to have had an effect. Jake wants her to be brought up by someone she knows and trusts, someone belonging to her, at least for a while. You didn't volunteer to take her on, did you?'

'Well, I can't have her. I'm too old to start bringing up a child all over again.'

'Exactly, and Jake's mother is crippled with arthritis, so that won't do, either.'

'Well, then, I don't suppose it will do any harm if you take over for a bit, at least until the child goes to school.'

Doris spoke grudgingly, and turned aside as the kettle began to whistle.

'Just let me know when you've made up your mind. We might want to let your room. I could do with some extra money coming in.'

That's all she cares about, Jenny thought bitterly. If she'd been a proper mother to me she wouldn't have let Ruth take Jake away from me. But she knew that wasn't fair. You couldn't force someone to love you, and once Jake had caught sight of Ruth, with her laughing ways, it was all over between him and Jenny.

Shrugging her arms into her navy blue winter coat she called over her shoulder to Doris.

'I'm just gong to pop round to see Rhonda.'

There was no reply. Jenny desperately needed to confide in someone who really understood, and Rhonda was the only one who knew her secret.

*   *   *

'You must be mad!'

Rhonda's green eyes opened wide as she wrapped her auburn curls in a towel, having just shampooed her hair.

8

The two girls were sitting in the kitchen of the pleasant semi where Rhonda still lived with her parents. Her father was at work and her mother had gone to the shops so they had the house to themselves.

'Oh, Ron, I thought you'd understand, at least.'

Jenny sniffed miserably into her damp handkerchief.

'Of course I understand, pet. I know how I felt when that fool of a Johnny Brown dumped me last year, but I got over it, and you will, too.'

'This is different, Ron. You know it is.'

With a little sigh, Rhonda settled back to listen, yet again, to the story she had heard so many times before. She was a gentle girl who understood that healing could only begin when Jenny managed to get rid of her feelings for Jake Thomas-Harding once and for all.

'Ruth managed to grab every one of my boyfriends when we were growing

9

up. Half the time she wasn't even in love with them. There was just something in her character that needed to prove she could win them away from me. Not that it took much doing,' she went on, twisting her handkerchief in her trembling hands. 'Nobody could resist Ruth. She was so alive and beautiful. Then once they'd fallen for her, she'd give them the push, and laugh about it afterwards. 'Men are so gullible,' she'd say.'

'And then you met Jake,' Rhonda prompted.

'And then I met Jake, on an outing of the birdwatchers' club. I had no idea, at first, that he was a wealthy man. He seemed so ordinary, dressed in hiking boots and comfortable, old clothes. He asked me for a date and we started going out on a regular basis. And then Ruth came home from college.'

Rhonda glanced at the clock.

'I'll have to set the table, and get the potatoes on. Mum and Dad will be in at any minute. Want to give me a hand?'

'Of course. Give me the spuds and I'll peel them for you.'

With her hands busy, Jenny felt calmer. Over the clatter of cutlery as her friend set the table she voiced her decision.

'So I've decided. I'm going to accept Jake's invitation to go and live at the Old Mill House.'

Rhonda dropped a fork.

'No, don't do that, Jenny. Jake will manage fine without you. The best thing you can do is to get right away from Elmhurst. Benson's have branches all over the country. Surely they'll give you a transfer. Make new friends, meet new people, find a new love. It's the only thing to do.'

'Is that what you did, after Johnny broke it off?'

Rhonda's face reddened.

'You know I didn't, but my home is here with Mum and Dad. I didn't do anything wrong. Why should I let that brute drive me away? As Mum says, the right man will come along one of these fine days, and the same goes for you, too, Jenny Doyle.'

Jenny washed the potatoes and put the pieces into the saucepan Rhonda provided.

'I know all that, Ron, but I've made up my mind. I'm going to the Old Mill House, and there's an end to it.'

'And is the idea that once he sees you every day over the breakfast table he'll realise what he's been missing, and you'll all live happily ever after? And what if it doesn't happen? You'll be worse off than before.'

'I love Jake. I've never stopped loving him, even when he was married to Ruth. Perhaps he never really loved me, probably he won't turn to me now, but at least I'll be able to see him. You know what they say, better half a loaf than no bread.'

Looking at the stubborn expression on her friend's face, Rhonda was deeply saddened. She was sure that Jenny was setting herself up for even more grief. She had done her best to talk her friend round, but she had failed. All she could do now was to be there for her when the crisis came, as it surely would.

2

The old mill house was a lovely old place, built from Cotswold stone. Strangers, who only knew it by reputation, sometimes had the idea that it must have been converted from a former mill, but this was not the case. It derived its name from the nearby flour mill which had been operated on the property long ago, but which was nothing but a ruin now.

The house itself, although far from being a stately home, was very much the dwelling of a Georgian gentleman. It had been built by some wealthy ancestor of Jake's mother. Jenny had no idea where their money had come from. She only knew that they were now involved in the wine-importing business.

When Jake and Ruth had been married, Robert Thomas-Harding had taken the opportunity of retiring, handing over the reins of business to his only son, along with the family's ancestral home. It was his hope that a grandson or two would come along in due course, to inherit the firm in their turn. But Ruth had been killed and there would be no sons, unless Jake chose to remarry. Meanwhile, Jenny meant to do the very best she could by her sister's little girl.

The house was bathed in sunlight as Jenny trudged up the gravelled driveway, wilting under the weight of her suitcase. Never having travelled to the house by bus before she had got off at the wrong stop and had to walk back. She felt warm in her winter coat and would have taken it off except that it would have meant something more to carry.

As she lifted the dragon's head door knocker and stood waiting, the enticing aroma of baking wafted towards her, making her mouth water. She had been too nervous to eat lunch but now she felt hungry. She rapped on the door a second time, and it was answered by Mary Gladstone, wiping her hands on an immaculate white apron.

'So sorry to keep you waiting, Miss Doyle. I'm alone in the house just now and I had to get my cakes out of the oven before they got too brown.'

'Do call me Jenny.'

'Aye, I suppose I could, seeing as you'll be living here from now on. And I'm Mary.'

She lifted the suitcase and quickly put it down again.

'My dear life, what have you got in there, bricks? Don't tell me you humped that all the way from the bus stop. But of course you did. Surely Mr Jake would have fetched you in the car this evening.'

'I wanted to come now,' Jenny said, trying to get a word in. 'I didn't want to wait until Sheena was in bed.'

'And now you've come, but she isn't here. Joan has taken her to a birthday party in the village, not that she wanted to go, poor child, but there you are! I suppose you'll be dying for a cup of something to keep you going until teatime, so just you leave that great case there and come down to the kitchen, and we'll see what we can find.'

While Jenny was seated at the kitchen table, sipping tea and sampling a fresh cake she listened with amusement as Mary Gladstone rattled on.

'Joan is my niece. She's a nurse at a big hospital in London, but she took time off to look after her mother, my sister, Gladys. All right now, she is, but had a nasty time of it. Joan will be glad you've come. She was just filling in here, of course. After poor Mrs Thomas-Harding was killed Mr Jake and I tried looking after young Sheena between us, but it was no life for a three-year-old. He has to go out to business, of course, and I have my work to do. Another cup of tea?'

Jenny noted that while she herself was to be called by her given name, her sister was referred to more formally as

Mrs Thomas-Harding. Was this an indication of what her position was to be in this house? What exactly had Jake said to Mrs Gladstone? As his sister-in-law, and Sheena's aunt, she was more than a hired nanny, but did he expect her to keep things on a more formal footing? She chided herself for being silly. People didn't stand on ceremony nowadays, did they? And Mary Gladstone was years older than herself.

As if reading her mind, the woman went on, 'I've known Mr Jake all his life, you know. I was cook here for his parents, and after my husband died they invited me to live in, and I've been here ever since. Gassed, my Norman was, in the Great War, and never really recovered. We never had children, else I wouldn't have been able to do it. Now, if you've finished your tea we'll go up and get you settled in.'

While Jenny had visited the house on several occasions in the past she had never stayed overnight and so had never had occasion to go upstairs. There was a very nice visitors' toilet on the ground floor, as well as the small sitting-room which had been Ruth's and her sister had never suggested showing her the rooms on the upper floors. Jenny had put it down to tact. She could not have borne to see the bedroom Jake shared with her sister.

Now she looked around her with interest as Mary Gladstone led her down a long hall, moving silently on her soft-soled shoes. They had reached another set of stairs and Mary Gladstone motioned to Jenny to go up. Jenny's heart sank. Visions of sparsely-furnished servants' quarters flashed before her eyes. She had seen too many television programmes full of maids and governesses who had to get up at the crack of dawn to attend to their duties. Sleeping under the roof, they had sweltered in summer and felt frozen in winter.

Mary chuckled.

'If you could see your face, Jenny! Young Sheena lives up here in the old nurseries, but you needn't worry. It was all modernised when Jake's parents got married. Everything is warm and snug, and you can use the nursery bathroom. We've put you in the room the nanny used to have because it's next door to the child and handy if you have to get up to her in the night. That's my little home there,' she went on, pointing to a closed door. 'I've a nice little parlour, and my own bathroom, leading off the bedroom. And here's where you go, Jenny.'

Jenny was saved from answering by shrieks of childish laughter and sound of pattering feet.

'Auntie Jen! Auntie Jen!'

The little girl flung her arms around Jenny's waist and then lifted them, wanting to be picked up. Jenny hugged her and swung her around. She felt a pang as she gazed at the child, who closely resembled Ruth as she had been at that age. She wore a white party frock with a wide blue sash, and hair ribbons which matched her blue eyes.

Her blonde hair had been allowed to grow long, and she looked less of a baby than she had done when Jenny had seen her last.

'And this is my niece, Sister Arkwright.'

'How do you do?'

'How do you do? But please, call me Joan.'

'And I'm Jenny.'

When Sheena had been carried off, protesting loudly, to have her clothes changed, Jenny ventured into her own room. It was very pleasant indeed, with walls distempered in pastel green, a thick green carpet, and matching curtains and bedspread in flowered chintz. Having bounced on the bed, she discovered that it was extremely comfortable.

The view from the window was pleasant, too. There were enormous lawns, and a glimpse of a stream in the distance. Probably that was the water which had powered the old mill, she thought. She must be careful when letting Sheena play outside.

She must fetch her case up and unpack while she had time to herself. Joan hadn't said when she planned to leave, but possibly she was eager to be on her way. When Jenny reached the main hall she heard the sound of a car on the gravelled drive. It was Jake. She stepped outside, eager to announce her arrival. She needed to speak to him about her plans for Sheena, feeling it was important to keep up the little girl's normal routine while avoiding any outside activities he felt unsuitable.

She moved out on to the stone steps as he came loping towards the house.

'Hello, Jake. I've arrived!' she said with a smile.

He paused briefly before pushing past her into the hall.

'I can see that, Jenny. I'm not blind! And there will be no need for you to meet me at the door every day like a dutiful wife. Is that clear?'

The welcoming smile froze on Jenny's face. Mary Gladstone had come down the stairs and to judge by the astonished look on her face, she had obviously heard the exchange of words.

'Hold my dinner back half an hour, will you, Gladdie? I've a number of important phone calls to make. Better not keep Sheena waiting, though. You can send their meal upstairs as soon as it's ready,' he said and disappeared in the direction of his study.

Jenny closed the front door carefully, although it would have relieved her feelings to have given it an almighty slam. How dare Jake speak to her in such an uncouth fashion? And she hadn't come downstairs on purpose to greet him. It would have served him right if he'd tripped over her suitcase.

'Come down to the kitchen with me, Jenny,' Mary Gladstone said quietly. 'We need to have a word about meals. Young Sheena has a lot of fads and fancies and I'll need to know whether you'll encourage that or not. I must say she's been allowed to run wild since Mrs Thomas-Harding died, poor little mite, and a wee bit of discipline won't come amiss.'

Jenny was still seething when they reached the kitchen. When they were seated at the table in the warmth of the Aga the older woman lowered her voice and said, 'Now, what was all that about? Mr Jake had no call to talk to you like that!'

Jenny shrugged.

'Don't ask me. I came down to collect my case, just as he drove in. I thought I might as well let him know I'd arrived, so I opened the door and hardly got a word out before he bit off my head.'

'Something went wrong at work, perhaps. He'll surely be all smiles and apologies later. Still, I'll have a word with him, point out the error of his ways.'

Jenny managed to smile.

'No, no, don't do that. As you say, he probably has things on his mind.'

'I'm off now, Auntie.'

Jane Arkwright came bustling into

the room, ending the discussion.

'Sheena's fallen asleep, but you may want to check on her later.'

'I'll go up now,' Jenny told her and, after being shown the workings of the dumb waiter, which would bring up her meal in due course, she left the two women to their goodbyes and slipped upstairs, lugging her suitcase with her.

Sheena was lying on top of her eiderdown, sound asleep, so Jenny went into the day nursery to set the table. After opening and shutting a few drawers she found cutlery and a checked tablecloth and set the table. That done, she went to the room allotted to her and began to unpack. Her blue leather writing case was on top of her neatly-folded skirts and blouses, and she took out the letter from Jake which had been read and folded many times.

My dear Jenny, he had written, *I am writing to ask a very great favour of you. Since my wife's death Sheena has naturally been quite unsettled and I'm anxious that life should return to normal for her, or as normal as it could be under the circumstances. She is fond of you, and of course you are her godmother. Could you find it in your heart to come here and take charge of her for the foreseeable future? I should be forever grateful.*

Yours ever, Jake.

It was a rather stilted letter, of course, too formal, and why had he referred to Ruth as 'my wife' as if Jenny was a stranger? She had put it down to the confused thinking of a bereaved husband, but now she was beginning to wonder if there had been something wrong between Ruth and Jake. If today's behaviour was anything to go by, perhaps he was a difficult person underneath the usually charming exterior.

'And perhaps that's all to the good,' she muttered.

Rhonda was probably right. She needed to put aside her feelings for her sister's husband, and move on. Except that she might never see Jake from one day to the next, if she was stuck up here, having all her meals in the nursery. So much for meeting him face to face over the breakfast table!

She wished now that she had listened to Gran and Doris, and stayed at home, setting out each day for work at the store where she enjoyed dealing with the customers in the ladies' wear department at Benson's, and having a few laughs with her co-workers at coffee break. She felt an overwhelming urge to throw her things back in her suitcase and rush out of this house of sadness, back to her own familiar surroundings, even if it did mean having to face Doris saying, 'I told you so.'

But then there was Sheena. She was genuinely fond of the child, and was serious about her responsibilities as godmother. There was no harm in sticking it out for a little while.

A fretful wail came from the next room, signalling that Sheena had come to life, and at the same time the distant sound of a buzzer indicated that the dumb waiter was on its way up, bringing their meal. Jenny thrust the letter back inside its hiding place, and went to attend to her duties.

3

'You don't look much like your sister,' Mary Gladstone said, with her head on one side. 'I mean, she was blonde and petite, and you are tallish and dark. Mrs Thomas-Harding had what is now called sex appeal, but you're the quiet type. No, I would never have taken you for sisters.'

It was a dull afternoon, cold for April, and Jenny was sharing a cup of tea with her new friend in what Mary called her parlour. It was a comfortable little room, furnished with armchairs and a small television set, and it had a small nook with a hotplate and the equipment for making tea. There was also a glass-fronted cupboard, filled with knick-knacks, its top smothered in what were obviously family photographs. A sepia picture of a man dressed in military uniform had pride of place — Mary's late husband, no doubt.

'That's because we're only half sisters,' Jenny said, keeping one ear tuned for any sound of Sheena, who was napping in her room down the hall. 'My mother died when I was only two, giving birth to my little brother, who lived only a few hours. I don't remember her, but I'm told that I resemble her quite a bit. Then Dad married Doris. I call her Mum but of course she's my stepmother, really. Ruth came along when I was four years old so we grew up thinking we really were sisters.'

'That explains it,' Mary said with a smile. 'I suppose Mrs Thomas-Harding took after her own mother.'

Jenny nodded in agreement, although Ruth's fairytale princess looks had always been a mystery to her family. Although Doris had a pleasant enough expression she could never be called anything other than plain. She was no oil painting, as Gran put it.

'I've a snap here you might be interested to see,' Mary said, getting up and selecting a framed picture from her display. 'Yes, that's Master James, as we all called him when he was small but at the time this was taken he started wanting to be called Jake. Mad about cowboys and Indians, he was, always reading books about them. Mrs Thomas-Harding senior always tried to steer him on to other books, Sir Walter Scott and John Buchan, all good adventure stories, but would he settle down to read them? He'd rather be rushing about on his pony, being Jake of Dead Man's Gulch, or such.'

Jenny took the photo and smiled to see the small boy, wearing a cowboy hat, holding a Shetland pony by the bridle.

'He didn't have a western saddle,' she remarked.

'Well, no, his parents wouldn't go that far, but they did come back from a trip to America with some cowboy boots for him, and a set of those things cowboys wear on their legs. Chaps, they call them. Of course, he outgrew that phase when he went off to boarding school. Which reminds me, he was saying something the other day about getting Sheena started on riding lessons soon.'

'Does she have a pony?'

'Not yet, but there's a very nice riding school not far away. You could take her there.'

'I'd enjoy that. I haven't ridden for a while, but it would be nice to be with horses again.'

Jenny was determined to speak to Jake about it. She had seen very little of him in the three weeks she'd been in the house. Was he deliberately avoiding her? After the awkwardness of that first day she'd kept her distance, too, but that was ridiculous. She'd done nothing wrong.

That evening, she went downstairs and knocked on the study door. Her heart fluttered when his deep voice commanded her to come in. He was seated at his desk, surrounded by books and papers.

'I don't mean to interrupt,' she began, but he flung down his pen and swivelled his chair around so that he sat facing her.

As he had done when she first met him, Jake was wearing old corduroys and a turtle-necked pullover. The smokey colour of the wool matched the deep blue of his eyes and went well with his black hair.

'Are you settling in all right?' he enquired.

'Yes, thank you,' she said primly.

No apology for the disgraceful way he'd treated her on that first day, she noticed, and no expressions of gratitude or acknowledgement of the fact that she'd dropped everything to come to his aid, put her life on hold, in fact! His arrogance annoyed her.

'Mrs Gladstone tells me that you'd like Sheena to have riding lessons,' she told him. 'Actually I'm quite a good rider, so I could teach her myself, if that's all right with you.'

'Certainly. You can take her into town and get her kitted out. See Miss Hopper for the money for shopping, but tell Marsh at the stables to send me a bill, all right?'

His eyes strayed back to his desk and Jenny felt that the interview was over. Thanking him, she left the room. She looked back as she closed the door but he was already frowning over his paperwork and seemed to have forgotten her.

Miss Hopper was the housekeeper. Recalling Ruth's boastfulness about her servants, Jenny had formed the impression that the woman was a formidable person who strode about the house wearing a bunch of keys on her belt and giving orders right and left! In fact, she was a tall, grey-haired woman with ill-fitting spectacles which she was forever pushing back from the middle of her nose, while sniffing peevishly.

She came to the house on a daily basis, Monday to Friday, and kept the house clean, although a woman came in twice a week from the village to do the tougher jobs. However, Miss Hopper was more than just a charlady. She did the shopping, dealt with the bills and presented cheques to Jake, ready for signing.

'And I know she'd like to live in,' Mary confided, 'but Mr Jake doesn't want that, although there's room enough in this house, goodness knows. She's a bit of a sourpuss, poor thing, but I suppose you can't blame her. Lost her whole family in the war, she did, in a bombing raid in London. Never married, so this place is her whole life, I suppose.'

Jenny looked forward to the riding lessons. With Mary and Miss Hopper dealing with all the household tasks there was nothing for her to do in the house, other than looking after Sheena, and she found the time dragged.

'Then why don't you take the child to that mother and toddler play group down the village?' Mary wanted to know. 'They meet three mornings a week and the kiddies play with their toys while the mothers enjoy a chat and a cuppa. Doesn't matter that you're not Sheena's mother. I know for a fact there's a granny who minds her daughter's child for her, and I did hear through the grapevine about a widower who takes his little boy along. Yes, you take Sheena to that. She needs to get to know other kiddies. Our Joan had quite a time with her when she took her to that birthday party. Hung back, the child did, refusing to muck in with the rest. It'll come hard on her when she goes to school, if she stays that shy.'

And so Jenny found herself walking down to the village hall, with Sheena dancing along at her side. The helpers greeted her pleasantly, as did the assorted mothers. Everything went well at first, discounting such minor crises as spilled orange juice and arguments over favourite toys. Then, when Sheena was quietly building a tower of blocks, carefully stacking one colourful plastic cube on top of another, she suddenly let out a howl of rage and burst into angry tears. A small boy had walked over and knocked the tower down, laughing with glee. Sheena ran to Jenny, burying her head in her aunt's skirts.

'Nasty boy!' she sobbed. 'Broke my house! He did it 'librately.'

The lone man in the group walked over and spoke quietly to the boy, who looked up at him, bewildered.

'I say, I am sorry,' he told Jenny. 'Is your little girl all right? Benjy didn't mean any harm. It's my fault, really. It's a game we play at home. He builds a high rise and then I come along with my wrecking ball and knock it down. Of course, he thinks it's great fun.'

Jenny smiled.

'I quite understand, and in any case, Sheena has to learn how to get on with other children. She hasn't had much experience up to now. She's been kept pretty close to home since her mother died.'

He raised one shaggy eyebrow.

'Oh, but I thought ... someone said ... '

'You thought I was Mrs Thomas-Harding? No, I'm her sister, Jenny Doyle. I've come to look after Sheena for a bit. She was very upset when Ruth died.'

'Naturally, she would be. Well, I'm glad to meet you, Miss Doyle, and I'm Seth Wilcox.'

'How do you do?'

One of the helpers stepped forward, clapping her hands.

'Story time, children! Mats, everyone!'

'This is when we have our cup of tea, Miss Doyle ... er ... Jenny,' Seth remarked, as the children scrambled to choose small mats and plumped themselves down in a circle.

After a moment's hesitation, Sheena joined in, while keeping a wary eye on young Benjy. Jenny found herself wedged in a corner, holding a mug of strong tea and hemmed in by Seth Wilcox on one side and a large, red-faced woman on the other. Like his son, Seth was no introvert, and both Jenny and her neighbour, who introduced herself as Annie's granny, found themselves listening to his patter.

He was a writer, he explained, which was fortunate because he was able to work at home and look after Benjy at the same time. Yes, he was a widower, and no, Benjy didn't miss his mother because she had died of cancer when he was just a baby.

'And what about you, Annie's granny? Is Annie's mother dead, too?'

The older woman giggled.

'No, she's very much alive. Works up at the grocery store. Her husband up and left her, and the three of us gets on very nicely together, thank you.'

Jenny and Seth exchanged grins. He seemed a likeable man, she thought. You couldn't call him good-looking, but there was something appealing about the combination of brown eyes and straight brown hair, coupled with an engaging smile. At the end of the session he tipped his hat and strode off, with Benjy dancing at his side.

'That boy's funny,' Sheena whispered.

'I thought you didn't like him.'

'When he broke my house, I hated him, Auntie, but when he blew bubbles in his juice, he was funny.'

'And when he was good, he was very, very good, but when he was bad, he was horrid,' Jenny quoted.

Surprisingly, Sheena hadn't heard the rhyme before, and it amused her. She skipped all the way home, chanting, 'When he was bad, he was howwid!' a sentiment which, as far as Jenny was concerned, could well be applied to Jake Thomas-Harding! She felt happier than she had done since her arrival at the Old Mill House. Sharing small talk with other adults had done her good. She really must try to get out more. Holding Sheena by the hand, she joined her in singing the nursery rhyme.

That evening, Rhonda phoned.

'Jenny! I've been wondering about

you. Listen, there's a really dishy new librarian at the library. A man!'

'And I suppose you think he'd be suitable for me, and you're about to fix us up?'

'Well, no,' Rhonda admitted. 'I've got my eye on this one for myself. Six feet tall, bright red hair and a deep voice. Totally irresistible! But I really called to ask about your own love life.'

'I met rather a nice man at the children's play group where Sheena goes. Seth Wilcox. He's a writer.'

Rhonda gave a squeal.

'Seth Wilcox! Not the man who writes those spy thrillers? Dad has every single one of them! And has he asked you out yet?'

'No, I've only just met the man. But you never know. He seems to be available and all the mums at the group are married women.'

There was a pause, and then, in a small voice, Rhonda asked about Jake.

'He's an absolute pig, Rhonda! I can't think what I ever saw in the man.

He's totally rude and grumpy. Poor Ruth must have had a very difficult time with him.'

'So you're cured of your infatuation then? Fallen out of love, have you?'

'If I haven't, I'm pretty close to it,' was Jenny's firm response, but Rhonda knew her too well.

'Are you sure of that?'

'Let's say I'm working on it. It's for the best, I know.'

And she refused to say another word on the subject.

4

Jenny was exhausted. During the day Sheena was a delight to be with, but she slept restlessly, often waking with nightmares. After one particularly bad night, during which she had awakened, screaming, Jenny felt that something had to be done.

'She was shouting, 'No! No!', Mary. I thought at first she was dreaming about Benjy, the little boy at play group who always knocks down her building blocks, but then she began calling, 'Mummy, Mummy.' I'm afraid she's reliving the accident.'

'That wouldn't surprise me at all,' Mary remarked, nodding wisely. 'It was a terrible smash, and who knows what Mrs Thomas-Harding might have said or done when she saw that lorry bearing down on them.'

Jenny winced. She had been haunted

by the thought of poor Ruth's last moments, before the bigger vehicle smashed into the driver's side of her little car.

'I'd have a word with Mr Jake, if I were you,' Mary went on. 'Perhaps the child should see the doctor.'

But when Jenny timidly approached him, Jake dismissed the idea at once.

'She doesn't need to see old Peters. What do you suppose he could do for her, anyway? I'm not having a three year old doped up with tranquillisers, so you can forget that.'

Intimidated by his angry glare, Jenny began to stammer.

'I didn't mean that. I thought he might recommend a child psychologist or something.'

'If you can't come up with something better than that, it's no use talking to you. The best thing to do is to tire her out during the day, then she'll sleep at night. Start on her riding lessons, take her to the zoo, I don't know.'

He turned away, and Jenny left the

room, furious. Why did he always make her feel like an idiot? And what kind of father was he, if he wouldn't seek professional help for his little girl? Perhaps if he spent more time with her, showed her some love and affection, that might help to settle the child.

'I'm doing the best I can,' Jenny muttered to Mary, 'but I'm just her aunt. She's too young to understand why her mother has left her. She needs to know that her father won't abandon her as well.'

'There's something in what you say,' Mary agreed. 'The thing is, I don't think Mr Jake is capable of showing love just now. He's frozen, like. Grieving over his wife's death. It's only natural.'

'He should be thankful his daughter survived the crash! I'm beginning to wonder if he resents Sheena because she's still alive, and Ruth's dead!'

Mary's mouth opened in shock and she put down the saucepan she was holding with a thud.

'That's a dreadful thing to say! Mr Jake would never think such a thing, never in this world!'

'Some people would.'

Jenny put her head in her hands and began to cry softly. Mary was at her side in an instant.

'What is it, love? What's happened? Come on, you can tell old Mary.'

'It was Doris, my stepmother. It was what she said just after Ruth died. I overheard her talking to a friend. I shouldn't have listened, but I couldn't help it. She said it wasn't fair that I was still alive when Ruth had been taken.'

Mary put an arm around Jenny's thin shoulders.

'There, there. Perhaps it was an awful thing to say, but once she'd stopped to think, I'm sure she was sorry she said it, and she never said it to your face, did she?'

Jenny shook her head.

'There you are, then. She doesn't wish you dead, any more than Mr Jake wants young Sheena out of the way.

And speaking of which, where is the child at this moment?'

'Helping Hoppy with the flowers.'

'Well, then, we've got a few minutes to ourselves. The kettle's just boiling. We'll have a nice cup of tea and you'll feel better. Nothing like a good, strong cup of tea to put the heart back in you.'

She bustled about, humming to herself, and when they were sipping their tea she went on.

'I've been thinking. You've been cooped up here ever since you arrived. You must be fair worn out. I tell you what. There's a new film at the Odeon, South Pacific, it's called. My friend Mavis went to see it, and she enjoyed it ever so much. You go along and see that tonight. Take you out of yourself.'

Jenny was doubtful.

'Jake hasn't said anything about my taking an evening off,' she began.

'Evenings off! Of course he hasn't said anything. You're a member of the family, not a servant. You pop along to the first house and I'll keep an ear open for young Sheena.'

'Perhaps I will.'

'That's all right then. And while we're on the subject of Sheena, why don't you ask Hoppy to move the child's cot into your room, just till she's over these nightmares? It would save you getting up and staggering down the hall half asleep. It might be a comfort to her, knowing you are there.'

Jenny felt comforted by Mary's home-spun wisdom. Her worries seemed to have dissolved like magic.

There was a long queue outside the cinema, but it was a pleasant evening and Jenny was in holiday mood and willing to wait her turn. Everyone else seemed in good spirits, looking forward to a pleasant evening's entertainment. She was trying not to notice a young couple who were very wrapped up in each other, when someone touched her elbow.

'Mind if I join you?'

It was Seth Wilcox!

'Er, I suppose not,' she said, and

then, feeling she'd been ungracious, she murmured something about his work, asking how he was getting on with his current book.

'Writer's block,' he replied cheerfully. 'Wanted something to take my mind off it, so here I am.'

Jenny was aware of some shuffling and grumbling among the people behind them, and she had a sneaking suspicion that Seth had used her as a means of jumping the queue. Still, it was pleasant to have a male companion while she waited. She half expected that, once inside the cinema, he would go his own way, but he stayed at her side as they followed the usherette down the aisle and slid into an adjoining seat.

In a way, this spoiled the film for her because she was keenly aware of his presence beside her, but apart from asking her if she wanted an ice-cream when the woman came past with her tray of refreshments, he ignored her.

'Not bad, was it?' he said, when they

followed the stream of people out into the cool, evening air. 'I thought the tunes were quite good, if you like that sort of thing. I prefer classical music myself.'

Jenny half hoped that he might offer to walk her home, or at least suggest they go to the café opposite for coffee, but all he said was, 'Well, I go this way,' and, tipping his hat, he strode off.

She made her way back to Old Mill House, wondering sadly if she was doomed to forever being treated by men as if she was part of the scenery. She wondered, not for the first time, why it was that some girls seemed to attract men like bees to a honey pot while others, such as herself, were overlooked. Without being unduly vain, she thought that she was reasonably attractive. She was hard working, she cared about other people and tried to be kind and polite. Didn't those things matter? But men seemed to want girls who could sparkle, and flirt, like Ruth. And Jenny wasn't interested in knowing how to flirt.

'Enjoy the film, did you?'

Mary Gladstone pushed her knitting into a clean pillowcase and went to put on the kettle.

'I'll make us a nice cup of tea, and then you tell me all about it. Mavis said the songs were ever so good.'

'I thought so, too. I'm going to see if I can get the sheet music, and try them out on the piano, if nobody minds.'

'Why should they? Do it good to be used again. Never been touched since Mr Jake's mother was here. Your sister didn't play, did she?'

No, Jenny thought. She was always too busy running here and there, driving the boys wild. I was the one who stayed home and practised scales because I had nothing else to do. Now, once again, I'll take out my frustrations on the piano keys. There was one particularly appropriate song in the film — I'm Gonna Wash That Man Right Out Of My Hair!

Sheena looked adorable in her tiny jodhpurs and hard hat. Mary Gladstone clapped her hands in delight at the sight of her.

'Oh, what a pity Mr Jake isn't here! He shouldn't miss this. Just you stay there, Sheena, pet, while I go and find my old camera.'

She bustled off to fetch her camera. Sheena looked down at her legs with satisfaction.

'Won't Daddy be surprised when he sees me riding a horse just like a big girl?' she lisped.

Jenny smiled.

'I expect he will, but you won't be able to ride all by yourself, you know. I'll be with you all the time.'

'Why?'

'Because a horse is a big, strong animal and I want it to walk slowly.'

'Why?'

Jenny was glad when they were interrupted by Mary, who took the child by the hand and marched her outside. It was nice that they would have a record of this important milestone in the child's life. Perhaps she would invest in a roll of film and borrow Mary's camera to photograph Sheena at play and she would buy an album to keep all the photos.

When they arrived at the stables, with Sheena clinging to Jenny's hand, they were greeted by a pleasant girl in breeches and a red polo jumper.

'I'm Anne Marsh. Dad told me you were coming, so I've saddled up old Prince. He's very quiet, perfect for young learners. You can take him into that ring over there. Do you want me to come with you?'

'No, thanks,' Jenny replied. 'I thought I'd teach her myself, though of course we won't be doing much today but getting her to feel comfortable in the saddle.'

Anne nodded, and led the way to where a small chestnut gelding was tethered to a ring in the wall.

'Up you go!'

Jenny boosted Sheena into the saddle and, having fitted the tiny feet into the stirrups and shown her how to hold the reins, they moved off slowly, with Jenny keeping a firm grip on the bridle.

'That's enough for today,' Jenny remarked, when, after half an hour or so had passed, they were back in the yard.

'No! No! Want to stay on!'

Prince's ears flicked back and Jenny moved swiftly to pluck the child out of the saddle. Prince might be placid enough, but even he would get excited if Sheena went into one of her foot-drumming tantrums.

'Sh! You'll frighten Prince.'

'Poor Prince,' the child said and caressed his neck lovingly.

'Having a lesson, are we?'

Jenny looked up, surprised to see Seth Wilcox looking down on her from a great height. The black gelding he was riding seemed to be at least seventeen hands tall.

'I didn't know you'd be here, Seth. Is Benjy with you?'

'No, no, he doesn't like horses. Had to get out for a bit of air, so I left him with the next door neighbour. Are you having lessons, too?'

Jenny explained that she could already ride, but was here for her niece's benefit.

'Then why don't you come out with me now?'

'I can't. As you can see, I've got Sheena with me.'

'Not a problem. Look, we'll go through the village and you can drop her off at home on the way, then we'll find some nice country lanes to trot around for a while.'

The offer was too tempting to refuse. Anne showed no surprise when Seth asked for another horse, and in no time at all Jenny found herself astride a pretty chestnut mare with a white blaze on its nose. They moved off down the street, with Seth holding Sheena firmly in front of him, Jenny having been unsure of her ability to control an untried horse and balance an active child at the same time. Sheena gazed about her in utter delight, looking happier than Jenny had seen her since her mother's death.

Jenny began to relax. It was good to be back in the saddle again.

Mary Gladstone came to the kitchen door, alerted by the sound of horses' hooves on the drive. She reached up to take Sheena.

'Come on, my girl, that's right. Had a nice time, did you?'

'Want to go with Auntie!'

She began to kick in Mary's arms.

'Tired out!' Mary mouthed, indicating with a wave that the riders should leave. 'You just come with me, Sheena, and see what I've got in the kitchen. Made them while you were gone, I did,' Mary went on and followed the scampering child into the house.

'Come on then, let's go before our time is up,' Seth declared, as his horse broke into a trot. 'Old Marsh is a bit of a stickler for time-keeping. Get back five minutes late and he charges you for another half hour!'

Jenny urged her mare into a canter and they flew down the drive, slowing when they reached the main road. Soon they were travelling through leafy lanes which were new to Jenny. Perhaps she should bring her bicycle from home and explore the surrounding country-side now that summer was coming. They were climbing a hill now, and after rounding a corner they drew their horses to a halt. Jenny gasped at the stunning panorama which stretched out before her eyes. The view was magnificent.

'I thought you'd like it. I often come here when I want a bit of peace and quiet,' Seth said.

Their horses were standing close together, cropping the grass. Jenny was aware of Seth's nearness as his leg momentarily brushed hers.

'We should do this more often,' he said, not looking at her.

'I'd like that, very much.'

He turned to her and smiled.

'All right, then, I'll give you a call and let you know when to meet me,' he told her.

A wave of irritation swept over her. Yes, she wanted to see more of Seth, but really, she wasn't prepared to dance to his tune! She already had one arrogant man to deal with, and now she was supposed to stand by, ready for orders from another one.

'By all means phone, and I'll let you know if I'm free,' she said coolly. 'I do have a child to think of, remember?'

A small smile of amusement altered the set of Seth's mouth. Perhaps he approved of her standing up to him.

'Come on, we must get back,' he said, wheeling his horse around.

They moved off down the hill, in perfect accord.

Mary Gladstone greeted Jenny with a knowing smile.

'Sheena's sound asleep on the kitchen settle. Worn out, poor lamb. You look pleased with yourself. Come and tell old Mary all about it.'

'Nothing to tell. We had a nice ride up to the top of a hill with a lovely view spread out down below.'

'Oh, yes? Lovers' Lane, they call that round here. Funny he took you up there on a first date, isn't it?'

'It wasn't a date,' Jenny insisted, blushing furiously. 'He was at the stables when we were there and he invited me to ride along, that's all.'

'So you won't be seeing him again, then?'

'Well, we might go riding again.'

'I thought as much,' Mary said triumphantly.

Jenny refused to dignify this with an answer, but she blushed again when Mary said, 'They've got them all in the library, you know, his books. Better read them, I'd say, then you can discuss them proper, like.'

'I hardly think we'll be discussing his books while we're out riding, Mary.'

'Ah, now, don't you scoff! Men are a

bit soft like that. You take an interest in what interests them and it flatters them, see? Makes them feel important.'

As far as Jenny was concerned Seth already possessed an overgrown sense of his own importance, but could it be that Mary knew what she was talking about? A memory came back to her of one of Ruth's cast-off boyfriends saying that when Ruth looked at you with those big blue eyes she made you feel like you were the most important man on earth.

Had Ruth made Jake feel that way? Jenny had loved him with all her heart but it was Ruth who had won him away from her. Perhaps she had a lot to learn.

5

'Come on, Sheena, you love scrambled egg,' Jenny said as she picked up a spoonful and waved it in her niece's direction. 'Here comes the train, down the little red tunnel!'

Sheena loved this game, although she was really too old for someone else to feed her, but on this occasion she turned her head aside fretfully. Jenny looked at her in concern, reaching across the table to feel her forehead. Carrying the child on her hip she hurried to find Mary Gladstone.

'Is there a thermometer in the house, Mary? She's burning up. I can't think what's the matter. She was all right at play group yesterday.'

'A bit of a cold, I expect,' Mary said comfortably. 'All sorts of germs going round down there, I don't doubt. Children pick up these things but they soon recover. She'll be right as rain tomorrow.'

She changed her tune when Sheena's temperature proved to be one hundred and two.

'I'd better phone Dr Peters and ask him to call in,' she said, shaking the thermometer back down. 'A nice wash, and then back to bed with that young lady, I'd say.'

'I'd better phone Seth,' Jenny told her. 'We were supposed to go riding this morning, but I'll be needed here now.'

When Seth finally answered the phone on the seventh ring, she thought he sounded irritated, but perhaps that was just worry.

'I was about to call you,' he announced. 'Young Benjy's just been sick as a donkey, all over the living-room carpet. Heaven only knows how I'll get that clean. I've just been putting him to bed and I'm waiting for Dr Peters to look in. I bet I know what he's going to say, though. There's measles in the village.'

Measles! Jenny had had that as a child, and she could remember the long, miserable hours spent in a darkened room. But perhaps in Sheena's case it was something else. She had a runny nose and was sneezing, but there was no sign of a rash.

She had just replaced the phone when it rang insistently.

'Old Mill House. Jenny Doyle speaking.'

'Oh, very lah-di-dah, I'm sure!'

Jenny's heart sank. Trust her stepmother to administer a put-down! Mary Gladstone had explained that Jake preferred members of the household to answer the phone in this manner. He often received business calls at home and, with several people in the house, a simple hello wasn't enough.

'Hello, Mum. How are you?'

'Not at all well. You'll have to come home and look after me. I tripped on the cobbles when I was hanging out the wash, and I've bruised my back. The doctor says I have to stay off my feet for a bit. How am I supposed to manage, I said, you tell me that.'

'What about Dad? Can't he give you a hand?'

'That'll be the day. Catch him with a dustpan and brush, I don't think.'

Jenny smiled ruefully. Doris was house-proud and the place always sparkled like a new pin.

'I meant he could make you the odd cup of tea and so on. Surely the house can look after itself for a bit.'

Doris seemed to be speaking between gritted teeth.

'We've let your room, Jenny. I've got the new lodger arriving tonight. As I said, you're needed here. Somebody has to get him his meals and do his washing and ironing. You can sleep on the settee. It will only be for a few nights.'

Jenny took a deep breath.

'I'm so sorry, Mum, I can't leave Sheena.'

'Bring her with you, then. It's a disgrace, the way those people have kept my only grandchild away from me.'

'Mum, please, listen. Sheena is ill. We're waiting for the doctor to come. That's why I can't leave now.'

'Nonsense. The housekeeper can look after her. I'll soon sort this out. Let me speak to my son-in-law.'

Jenny was glad to be able to say that Jake wasn't at home. Closing her ears to further threats she said a firm goodbye and put down the phone. She hoped that Doris would think better of phoning back later. Would Jake insist that she, Jenny, should return home? He had been so cold and distant since her arrival that she wondered if he regretted asking her to come. And if he did use this as an excuse to send her away, what lay ahead of her at her old home? Her room was let to a stranger, and her job was gone. She wondered miserably if Benson's would let her have it back.

Dr Peters confirmed that Sheena had measles.

'But she doesn't have a rash, Doctor,' Mary Gladstone protested.

'That should make its appearance on the fourth day,' he replied. 'If you can get this young lady to open her mouth again you'll see that she has white spots inside her cheeks, a sure sign of measles, I'm afraid.'

Beckoning to the two women to follow, he led the way out of the room and proceeded to give directions as to how they should care for the child.

'It's complications we have to watch for, in a child this age. Pneumonia, possible eye damage and so on, but we won't let it come to that.'

'Dear, oh dear,' Mary quavered. 'I wish Joan was here. She'd know what to do.'

'You'll do well enough if you follow my instructions and I'll call again tomorrow.'

Jake took his daughter's illness in his stride, accepting Mary's explanation that all children caught various diseases once they mingled with others of their own age.

'And if she hadn't come in contact with it at the play group, she'd have caught it later, when she started school, the doctor says.'

Sheena greeted her father hoarsely, demanding to be read to, and Jenny was pleasantly surprised when he picked up her well-worn copy of Beatrix Potter's Tom Kitten and began on the adventures of the naughty, little cat. It was the first time she'd seen him taking an active interest in the child. Perhaps he wasn't as uncaring as he seemed.

Everything changed when the rash emerged. Not one part of the poor child's body was spared and her eyelids were swollen and heavy.

'Light hurts my eyes, Auntie,' she said plaintively, even though Jenny had pulled the curtains shut.

At the direction of the District Nurse, who called in each morning on her rounds, Mary kept a steam kettle boiling, and Jenny rubbed camphorated oil on Sheena's back and chest. But her temperature rose alarmingly and she was so fretful that it was almost impossible to get her to swallow the fluids ordered by the doctor.

'I think you should come,' Jenny told Jake that night. 'Her temperature's almost one hundred and five. That's dangerous, isn't it?'

'I'd better call Peters.'

But the doctor's wife told him that her husband was out on a maternity case and she couldn't say when he might be back. All she could suggest was that they sponge Sheena down with cold water.

Jenny and Jake watched as Sheena tossed and turned throughout the night. It broke Jenny's heart to hear her calling for her mother.

'Mummy, Mummy! I want my mummy!'

Jake sat with his head in his hands. Jenny could only imagine what was going through his mind. She wrung out a flannel and bathed the hot little head.

'I'm here, darling. Try to go to sleep now.'

That seemed to comfort the child, who lay staring up at the ceiling. Mary Gladstone poked her head around the door and said in a whisper that she was making tea and would anybody like some? Jake shook his head.

'Yes, please,' Jenny said, 'and you must try to take something, too, Jake. You haven't eaten today. I'm sure you could swallow a bit of toast.'

Mary nodded, and disappeared. Jake looked up at Jenny with a mute appeal in his eyes.

'I know,' she told him, 'this is worrying but I'm sure she'll be all right soon.'

'I can't bear it if anything happens to her,' he muttered. 'She's all I've got left.'

Jenny felt like crying. He must have been so much in love with Ruth. How could she ever have thought that he might turn to her instead?

The night passed slowly, every minute seeming like an hour. Jenny had all but fallen asleep in her chair when she was roused by the peeling of the front door bell. She heard Mary pattering down the stairs and moments later Dr Peters appeared.

'Couldn't get here earlier, delivering twins!' he announced. 'Let's have a look at this young lady then, shall we?'

Jenny could hardly believe it when he announced that the fever was broken and that Sheena was on the mend.

'She'll have to stay in bed for a couple of weeks yet, of course,' he went on, 'and she still needs careful nursing, which I'm sure you can manage, Miss Doyle, but she's turned the corner, as they say. I'm off home to breakfast now. Can see myself out.'

He went downstairs, whistling cheerfully. Jake and Jenny stood at the top of the stairs and watched him go. Overwhelmed with happiness and relief, and too exhausted to be aware of what she was doing, Jenny enveloped Jake in a bear hug. Automatically his arms went round her as he stooped to kiss her. What began as an affectionate embrace deepened into a passionate kiss to which Jenny eagerly responded. Joy welled up in her and it was as if they had never been apart.

They had been together like this before he had abandoned her in favour of her sister, leaving Jenny hurt beyond belief and wondering how she would ever find the strength to go on. But the years of unhappiness were behind her now, swept away in one time-stopping moment, and they were together again. And this time she would never let him go. Nobody would ever be allowed to come between them again.

Her joyful dream was shattered when Jake broke loose from her arms and stepped back abruptly, almost falling on to the top stair as he did so.

'I'm sorry!' he muttered. 'I can't do this, Jenny, I'm sorry!'

Then he turned on his heel and marched off to his room, leaving her standing alone, asking herself what had gone wrong.

6

Jenny did find an opportunity to visit her stepmother but had received a cool reception. Despite having been visited each day by the District Nurse and temporarily allotted the services of a home help, Doris was bitterly resentful of Jenny's failure to rush to her side in time of need. She barely paid attention to the report of her granddaughter's progress and sat restlessly in her chair, looking grim. When a friend arrived at the door, Jenny seized the opportunity to make her escape, explaining that she had promised to meet Rhonda for coffee.

Rhonda was full of news about her new boyfriend, the librarian, Peter Steele.

'He really is the perfect man,' she enthused, sighing happily.

'That's what you used to say about

Johnny Whatsisname,' Jenny reminded her.

'Oh, him!'

Rhonda dismissed the forgotten Johnny with a wave of her hand.

'I must have been mad to fancy him. Of course, I was younger then and didn't know what I was doing. No, Jenny, this is the real thing, I'm sure of it. Peter knows so much about every-thing, but he's not arrogant with it. So down to earth and considerate, and we seem to agree on a lot of things.'

'Lucky you.'

'That's what I think. But what about you? Sheena is on the mend, I take it, or you wouldn't be here.'

'Yes, she's at the grumpy stage now. The rash has gone but she's supposed to stay in bed for another week or so and she's bored to tears. Even her favourite books don't appeal, and if I have to play one more game of snakes and ladders, I'll scream.'

'And what about the delectable Jake? Any progress there?'

'Oh, Ron, it's all such a muddle Perhaps I shouldn't say anything. I really don't know where to start.'

'Now, none of that, you can tell your Auntie Ron.'

'Well, we'd been up for a few nights with Sheena. She really was quite ill for a time, and we were both exhausted. Her temperature went up to a hundred and five, Ron, and Mary Gladstone kept saying she hoped it wouldn't go any higher, or there could be brain damage. You can imagine how that made us feel! Anyway, Dr Peters dropped in one morning and told us that Sheena was over the worst and should get better without any complications. I don't quite know how it happened, but the next minute Jake and I were in each other's arms. I was deliriously happy, as you can imagine.'

'So that's good, isn't it?'

'That's the problem. He suddenly pushed me away, telling me he was sorry and hadn't meant to do it. He rushed off somewhere and I haven't seen him since.'

'So now what?'

'You tell me. I feel I'm worse off than before. I'd have sworn he still has feelings for me, but maybe as he says, it was a mistake. I keep telling myself that we were tired and stressed and weren't really in our right minds. At least, I was,' she finished sadly.

'I suppose you'd better make the most of your friend, Seth Wilcox, then.'

'What's he got to do with it?'

'Well, if Jake has any feelings for you at all, and he thinks you're interested in someone else, it might bring him to his senses.'

'I'm not going to use Seth, if that's what you have in mind.'

Rhonda clucked her teeth in exasperation.

'You're already going out with the man, aren't you?'

'Yes, just as friends.'

'There you are then. How is that using him, unless this friendship can help take your mind off Jake? Don't

75

be so wet, Jenny.'

The friends soon said their goodbyes and Jenny headed home.

'You're back, Auntie!' Sheena cried, holding up her thin little arms to Jenny. 'I missed you. Where have you been?'

'I went to visit your Grandma Doyle,' Jenny explained. 'She hasn't been very well, either.'

'Did she have the measles, too?'

'No, no, she slipped on the stairs and twisted her ankle.'

'Oh. Did she send me anything?'

'No, she hasn't been able to get out to the shops, but I've brought you something.'

'Goody, goody! What is it?'

'Open the parcels and see.'

The first one contained a book.

'Read it to me now.'

'Perhaps later. Open the other parcel.'

Sheena was enchanted with the kaleidoscope it contained. Jenny showed her how to use it and the child was thrilled with the bright patterns it produced.

Mary Gladstone put her head round the door.

'That Mr Wilcox phoned while you were out. Told me to say his little boy is much better, so if you want to go riding tomorrow, he'll be at the stables at ten.'

'Thanks, Mary. I'll think about it.'

'You go. You've been cooped up here so long your face is quite pale. Do you good to get out in the air.'

'Is Jake at home?'

Jenny hated herself for asking, but she couldn't help herself.

'Oh, I forgot to tell you. He's gone to France.'

'France!'

'Yes, on business, of course. Something about seeing a new vineyard. It all happened in a hurry because he came rushing in, packed a bag and dashed off to catch a plane. Back on Wednesday, he said.'

'Say the rhyme, Auntie, say the piggledy rhyme,' Sheena pleaded.

Jenny obliged.

'Higgledy piggledy, my fat hen . . .'

'I do love you, Auntie Jen. I love you best!' the little girl said delightedly when the rhyme was ended.

Jenny was touched.

'Don't you love Daddy best?'

''Course I love him best in the world, and I love you best, too.'

With a lump in her throat, Jenny knew that she had to stay on here as long as she was allowed to, no matter how hard it was for her to live alongside Jake. She also knew that she mustn't usurp her sister's place in Sheena's small world. When the time was right she must find some photos of Ruth and perhaps talk to Sheena about her mother. It would help to keep Ruth's memory alive in her little girl's heart.

* * *

Mary Gladstone came to Jenny, all agog.

'There's been a phone call from Mr Jake. We're to give a big party next week. Oh, I am looking forward to it.

We've been so quiet here since his poor wife died. It will be lovely to have the house full of people again.'

'What sort of party? Friends and neighbours?'

Jenny wasn't sure how she would feel about entertaining people from Jake's and Ruth's social circle. She was sure they'd all be trying to size her up as Ruth's less attractive, older sister, and whispering among themselves as to her exact relationship with Jake! But Mary shook her head.

'No. It's something to do with clients of the firm. It's to be a wine-tasting evening, apparently. I hope I get a look in. I hear it's a very funny sight. They take a sniff, then a mouthful, swill it around, and then they spit it out! Can you imagine such a thing, with expensive wine like that? As a girl I always understood it was rude to spit.'

'I don't think it's quite like that, Mary,' Jenny told her, although she had to admit that she wasn't too sure of the procedure either.

'Anyhow, Mr Jake is leaving it all to us. I'm to see to the food, of course. I have to serve them bits of apple in between glasses of wine, to clear the palate, whatever that may be when it's at home. Then there'll be eats and coffee when the tasting is over. Can't have them all driving away cross-eyed. Hoppy will make sure all the best crystal is washed and polished, and if you want to make yourself useful you can do some nice flower arrangements. If there isn't enough in the garden you can order more from the flower shop, Mr Jake says.'

It all sounded like fun. Trust Mary to reduce it all to the status of a children's tea party! Jenny hoped she'd be invited to take part. She knew next to nothing about wines, but would like to learn.

On the day of the party the house was a bustle. Sheena, up and about for the first time, scampered about, getting under everyone's feet. Since her illness she seemed to have sprouted up, looking taller and thinner. Her toddler baby fat was gone, leaving a very grown-up looking little girl.

Jenny had just placed a huge vase of flowers on the sideboard and was standing back to admire the effect when the doorbell rang. She heard the murmur of voices as Mary greeted the visitor, and then a strange, young woman stalked into the room and stood, hands on hips, eyeing Jenny up and down. Intimidated, Sheena dodged behind Jenny and peered out at the newcomer.

'This is Miss Doyle,' Mary said, looking flustered, 'and this is Miss Magda Hall. She's Mr Jake's personal assistant at work.'

'How do you do?'

Instead of responding to Jenny's greeting, the newcomer turned to Mary and said, 'That will be all, thank you. If I need you again I'll call you.'

Dismissed, Mary went back to the kitchen, closing the door none too gently behind her. Jenny instinctively mistrusted Magda Hall. The woman was dressed to the nines in a smart suit and four-inch heels, and there was not a hair out of place in her smooth chignon. Clearly, she spent a great deal of money on her appearance, but perhaps that was expected of her, working as she did in a rather up-market job.

Dressed in her working garb of shabby slacks and well-worn pullover, Jenny towered over the petite Miss Hall and felt gawky by comparison.

'Can I help you at all?' she ventured.

'I'm just here to make sure that everything is properly set up. Mr Thomas-Harding is a stickler for protocol, as perhaps you know. However, I don't think this is the place for little Sheila, is it? Not with all this expensive crystal sitting about. Why don't you run along, dear, and take your governess with you?'

This was too much. The time had come for Jenny to assert herself.

'We're quite all right here, thank you, Miss Hall. And Sheena, as she is called, is a very careful child, and this is her first day up and about after having measles. Since I haven't finished doing the flowers yet, I want to keep her with me. And I'm not the governess, as you put it. I'm your employer's sister-in-law. Ruth was my younger sister.'

Magda Hall was not at all abashed, obviously not at all embarrassed by her gaffe, although her manner changed slightly. She moved about, rearranging things on the sideboard and counting the silverware.

'I must have a word with your cook before I go. Is she up to the job, Miss Doyle? I wanted to bring in outside caterers but Mr Harding insisted that the woman is competent.'

'I should jolly well think she is!' Jenny said, coming to Mary's defence. 'She's been with the family since before Jake was born. His parents would hardly have kept her on if she was incompetent.'

'I suppose not. Now, where is the housekeeper? I need a word with her.'

'I'm afraid she's not here at the moment. May I help?'

'I'd like to see over the house. I suppose you can give me the guided tour.'

Jenny misunderstood.

'The guest toilets are just down the hall, and there's a good-sized cloakroom with racks for coats. Jake's parents used to entertain a lot and I understand that was one of their innovations.'

'But the rest of the house. I would like to see that.'

This was a strange request, Jenny thought. Surely one didn't come to the home of one's boss and insist on acting as if the place was up for sale! The other woman noticed her slight frown and answered calmly.

'I'm sure your brother-in-law wouldn't mind, Miss Doyle. After all, I may be coming to live here some day, so I do think I have the right to see what I'm getting into.'

Jenny froze. Was there something more between Jake and his assistant than a business relationship? Could this be why he had recoiled so suddenly from his embrace with Jenny? Her gaze flew to the woman's left hand but there was no sign of a ring. All this time Sheena had been standing quietly at Jenny's side, but now her thumb plopped out of her mouth and she said in ringing tones, 'Don't like that lady.'

'What a rude little girl!' Magda Hall remarked, her voice dripping with ice. 'When I come to live here I shall have to teach you better manners.'

'You'll have to excuse Sheena,' Jenny snapped. 'As I said, she's been very ill and she's still not quite herself. I suggest you ask Miss Hopper to show you around the house. She should be back at any moment.'

Without further ado, she then took Sheena by the hand and swept out of the room.

'Don't like that lady!' Sheena said again.

'Neither do I,' Jenny agreed, under her breath. 'Neither do I.'

85

7

Seth Wilcox phoned unexpectedly several days later, catching Jenny quite unawares.

'I've a big favour to ask, Jenny. Thing is, I'm in a bit of bother. I have to go to London to see my editor, something about a plot line that doesn't quite work, according to him. Anyway, it's Benjy. I can't take him with me, of course, and the woman who usually babysits is tied up with her own child, who now has measles. Is there any possibility you can help me out? I'll only be away for the day.'

Jenny hesitated. Did she really want to get involved?

'I'll stand you a nice dinner as a reward,' he pleaded, and she laughed.

'Why not bring Sheena?' he said. 'The pair of them can play together, and if I'm late returning home you can put her to bed in the spare room. Oh, I'm not asking you to stay overnight,' he added hastily. 'I'm picking up my sister, and bringing her back for a short visit, so I can run you home in the car while Jessie stays with Benjy.'

So the next day, Jenny found herself in Seth's cottage.

'Make yourself at home,' Seth said, as the two small children stared at each other shyly. 'Feel free to look around, but please don't let the kids touch anything in my study. Benjy knows he's not allowed to meddle, but he's only three, after all. Forbidden fruit and all that.'

Jenny was rather interested to see how a real writer lived, so when he had gone, she peeped into the study, but apart from a packed bookshelf it was rather like any ordinary office. A flat-topped desk held a battered type-writer and mounds of paper and a large steel filing cabinet stood nearby. One shelf held Seth's publications and she was impressed to see how many books he had actually written. The day passed quickly. At eight o'clock Jenny insisted that the children should go to bed. Benjy protested loudly, begging to hear his favourite record just one more time.

'Daddy lets me,' he added, with a sly grin.

'Daddy isn't here,' Jenny replied, as she took him upstairs and got him into his pyjamas.

That done, she settled Sheena in the spare room, although the child was uneasy and begged her aunt not to go away. Jenny stayed with her until, thumb in mouth, she fell asleep. It was quite late when Jenny heard the car pulling up outside the cottage. She stood on the doorstep while Seth helped his sister out of the car, and went to the boot to retrieve her suitcase.

'Jessie, this is Jenny Doyle. Jenny, my sister.'

Jessie was a stout, cheerful woman, clearly some years older than her brother.

'My, that was a long trip! I could murder a cup of tea,' she announced.

Jenny went through to the kitchen to put on the kettle.

'I'll take your case upstairs in a while,' Seth said. 'Sheena is in the spare room, I take it? No point waking her till you're ready to leave.'

'I must go soon, though,' Jenny pointed out, although really there was no good reason why she had to return to the Old Mill House immediately and Jessie had said she was tired and was probably longing for her bed.

Two days later, Jenny was down in the village, doing some shopping for Mary Gladstone, when she encountered Jessie in the butcher's.

'Want to come for a coffee, Jenny? My feet are fair killing me.'

She waited while Jenny bought and paid for her purchases and then the pair sauntered down to the tea-room where half the village seemed to have congregated for morning coffee.

'Quick! There's a table over there!'

Jessie said, squeezing past some departing customers and sitting down. 'A pot of coffee, please, and a selection of pastries,' Jessie directed the harassed waitress.

Jenny was amused. She was just like Seth, who always assumed that he was the only one whose wishes counted and who never thought to consult the other person! Still, she herself wanted coffee and pastries, so there was no point in raising a protest.

'Now!' Jessie commanded, when they had distributed their packages under the table and were waiting for their food to arrive. 'Tell me all about yourself! Seth tells me that you are looking after little Sheena because your sister died. You're here by yourself, so where is the little one today?'

She rattled on, and it was some time before Jenny could get a word in. Jessie had more questions. How long would Jenny be staying, did she have a career to go back to, and so on? All in all it was more like a job interview than a friendly chat, Jenny thought, but she replied politely all the same. There was something likeable about Jessie.

'I suppose you'll go back to your job when your brother-in-law remarries?'

'What? I'm sorry, Jessie, I was thinking of something else,' Jenny blurted out, playing for time.

The older woman frowned.

'Your brother-in-law, Mr Thomas-Harding, isn't it? Surely you knew. I understand he's about to announce his engagement. Oh, I am sorry if I've spoken out of turn. You must be missing your sister, of course. It can't be easy for you to see him preparing to marry someone else.'

You don't know the half of it, Jenny thought.

The blood was pounding in her ears and she spoke carefully, trying not to show her feelings.

'You seem to know something I don't. What, exactly, have you heard?'

'I heard it from Mrs Metcalfe, who cleans for Jake. She works part time at the Red Lion and she just happened to be dusting in Reception when this woman came in, all red nails and smart hairdo, a real townie, I'd say. Well, she had come there to book rooms for herself and two businessmen. There was to be a fancy do up at the Old Mill House, she said, drinking a lot of wine, and nobody wanted to risk driving home the worse for wear.'

'Sounds reasonable to me,' Jenny said, realising Jessie was referring to Jake's wine-tasting evening.

'Yes, but apparently she went on to say that she was sure they'd give her the best possible service, as she was the fiancée of Mr Jake Thomas-Harding of the Old Mill House. But, according to Mrs Metcalfe, there was no sign of an engagement ring. Perhaps they made the announcement at the big party, up at the house.'

Jenny became aware that Jessie was staring at her with interest.

'Well, is that what they did? You were there, surely?'

'No, I don't think anything was said.'

She cast her mind back. She hadn't been invited to take part, but then, why should she have been? It was a business event, not a private party. However, unobserved by those below, she had watched part of the proceedings from the small balcony, which was reached from an upper floor. The dining-room and an adjoining reception area were divided by a panelled partition which could be folded back to make one huge, lofty-ceilinged room for special occasions.

With an aching heart Jenny had watched the scene below, curious to see what happened at a wine-tasting. Jake was devastatingly handsome in evening dress, while Magda, clad in a ballet-length gown of flame chiffon with a plunging neckline, dogged his footsteps. She seemed very much in her element, playing the part of hostess as to the manner born.

Jenny hadn't spent the entire evening on the balcony, of course. From time to time she had gone to check on Sheena, who was sound asleep in her room. However, when the main purpose of the evening was over, Mary Gladstone, regal in a black dress and spotless white apron, had circulated with trays of food, accompanied by Hoppy. Had there been an announcement of any kind she would have heard it, and undoubtedly mentioned it to Jenny the next morning.

'No, Jessie, I'm sure nothing was said, but this was a business event for Jake's clients, hardly the place for personal announcements,' Jenny said coming back to the present.

Jessie grunted.

'Oh, well, we'll find out all in good time, I suppose. Seems funny to me that your brother-in-law hasn't said anything, though. I mean, where does this leave you?'

In the dust, Jenny felt like saying. Once married to Jake, Magda wouldn't tolerate having his former sister-in-law in the house, and Jenny certainly couldn't bear to watch the two of them together.

'You'll have to find yourself a husband, then.' Jessie smiled. 'You don't want to put it off too long, or you'll find yourself left on the shelf, like me!'

Jenny went straight home and looked for Mary Gladstone. She knew she shouldn't betray her emotions to the woman who, after all, owed her loyalty to Jake, but she was so distraught she couldn't help herself. Mary was in the kitchen, stirring something in a pan on the cooker, and Sheena was busy at the table, rolling out a very grubby piece of dough.

'Look, Auntie Jenny, I'm making biscuits.'

'Lovely. Are you going to let me taste one?'

'Not yet, silly. They have to cook first.'

'Oh, I see. Mary, I need to talk to you.'

Mary smiled ruefully.

'I should just think you do. You've a face like a wet weekend. Well, out with it, then!'

Jenny glanced at Sheena.

'It's about Jake,' she whispered.

'Oh, yes, what's he done now, then?'

'Apparently got himself engaged to Magda Hall.'

'What!'

In her agitation, Mary dropped her wooden spoon on the floor and Jenny rushed to turn down the gas under the bubbling soup before it boiled over. Harmony restored, Mary asked her what on earth she meant. Jenny repeated what she had heard, second hand, from Jessie Wilcox, but Mary denied everything stoutly.

'Wishful thinking! If there was anything like that in the wind I'm sure you-know-who would have told me. Not that he has to ask my permission, mind you, but I've known him a lot longer than she has, the hussy. He often says that I'm like a second mother to him.'

'But, Mary, she did hint at something when she was here the day before the party. She wanted to see over the house, something about wanting to make changes.'

Mary sniffed.

'I've heard of women like her, secretaries and that, who've been with their bosses so long they think they own them. Thinks a lot of herself, does that one. You heard the way she spoke to me. *You can go back to your kitchen now, you're not wanted here.* Well, the day that one moves in here is the day I move out!'

She turned back to the stove, bristling.

As she helped Sheena to arrange her biscuits on a greased baking sheet, a thought occurred to Jenny. There were plenty of unoccupied bedrooms in the house, so if Magda was Jake's future wife, why had she stayed at the Red Lion? It couldn't have been for the sake of her reputation. With three other women and a child on the premises she would have been well chaperoned.

A small flicker of hope flared up in Jenny's heart.

8

'What about that dinner I promised you?' Seth asked when Sheena and Jenny arrived for their next regular appointment at the stables.

Sheena had missed her riding lessons and was keen to get started again, and Jenny wanted to build up her confidence.

'I'm not sure.'

'Oh, come on, now's our chance, while Jessie is here to babysit. There's a new restaurant in Norton I'd like to try, but it would have to be egg and chips at the greasy spoon if Benjy had to tag along with us.'

'All right then, I'd love to.'

So Wednesday evening saw Jenny in Seth's elderly car, speeding to the nearby town. He was an erratic driver and she found herself clutching the hand strap, trying not to show her alarm. She was thankful when they arrived at the restaurant, and she refused to spoil her evening by dwelling on the hazards of the return journey, although, if Seth happened to have too much to drink, she was quite prepared to go home by bus!

The Golden Hind was very swish indeed. Summing up Seth as a down-to-earth fellow she had half-expected a room filled with red-checked tablecloths and candles stuck into old wine bottles, but she was wrong. Dark-panelled walls, hung with old hunting prints, muted lighting, linen napery and real flowers on the tables made for a most pleasant atmosphere. And she was taken aback to find that the menu handed to her by a charming waiter had no prices on it. What on earth was she to do? She had no idea what Seth could afford and had a horrid vision of them up to their elbows in soap suds, doing the washing up to pay for their meal!

'I'll order for us both, shall I?' he asked.

'Yes, please do. I don't have any particular dislikes.'

For once she was glad of his take-charge behaviour. It was rather nice to sit back and relax, enjoying the pleasant surroundings and she was impressed when a trio took their places in a corner of the room and began to play light, classical music. They had just finished their vichyssoise, and were waiting for their veal scaloppini, when some new diners were ushered in and seated at a nearby table. Jenny froze. It was Jake and Magda, both dressed to kill, and obviously out on the town together.

'Anything wrong, Jenny?' Seth asked.

'What? Oh, nothing. My brother-in-law and a friend have just come in, that's all.'

'Shall I ask them to join us?'

'No, Seth. His friend is someone I don't like very much and I don't want our lovely evening spoiled.'

'Good. Just as well, then, because I have something I want to ask you.'

He leaned forward and refilled her wine glass.

Then, not meeting her gaze he mumbled, 'We get on well together, I think. I mean, we like each other, don't we?'

Startled, and wondering what was coming next, Jenny replied, 'Yes, I suppose we do.'

'And I think we make a good team. We have similar interests, and so on. And I know you like young Benjy, and he's certainly taken a shine to you. What I'm trying to say is, will you marry me, Jenny?'

'What? Oh, Seth, I don't know what to say,' she stammered, resisting the urge to come out with the old Victorian cliche, this is so sudden! 'I mean, we haven't known each other very long, and I don't know if I'm ready to settle down yet.'

This was not at all how Jenny had imagined her first proposal of marriage would be, and it was all wrong! She had the candlelight, the wine, the soft music, but the love of her life was sitting across the room with another woman. Even as she watched, Magda leaned across to Jake to whisper something in his ear. Her hand, with its long, red fingernails rested on his shoulder and he did not recoil from her touch.

Jenny's attention snapped back to Seth, who was saying something about Benjy needing a mother and how he felt that it wasn't good for the boy to be an only child. She nodded politely and he seemed to take this for encouragement and bounced back to his old, confident self.

'No need to give me your answer tonight,' he went on. 'I'm sure you'll want to speak to your parents and so on, and if you want me to call on your father to ask his permission, I'm quite willing to go along with that. However, we shouldn't leave it too long. I have to go to Venice fairly soon for background research for my new book, and if we were married in time that could be our honeymoon.'

Part of a package deal, she thought bitterly.

She barely tasted the rest of the meal and was further downcast when Jake, apparently going to the gent's, passed by their table and saw the pair of them sitting there. With contempt in his dark eyes he strode on by, and there was no chance for Jenny to introduce him to Seth, who had noticed nothing.

★　★　★

'So that's where it stands,' Jenny told Rhonda, having rushed to talk to her friend the next afternoon.

Rhonda sighed happily.

'I'm glad for you, Jenny, I really am. Now, if I could just bring Peter to the point, we could have a double wedding. Imagine the pair of us together at St Margaret's, up to the ears in white satin and lace, carrying bouquets of orange blossom.'

'This is no joking matter, Ron! Seth made it sound like a business arrangement. Where's the romance in that?'

'We're not schoolgirls any longer, Jenny, saving up our pennies to buy the latest Elvis Presley and drooling over lads from the boys' grammar school! Perhaps the French have the right idea, viewing marriage as a business arrangement, like you said.'

'I thought Frenchmen were supposed to be so romantic.'

'I'm sure it's possible to have both. As I see it, you're on to a good thing. Venice for a honeymoon! And you say he has a nice little cottage, and he must have a good income from all those best-sellers. I wouldn't mind being in your shoes, I can tell you.'

'It can't be right to marry a man when you're in love with someone else.'

'Jake is just a fantasy. You've got to face up to the fact that he's not in love with you, and never will be.'

Then why had he seemed so furious when he'd seen her in the restaurant with Seth? Gran would call him a dog-in-the-manger. He didn't want Jenny for himself but he didn't want anyone else to have her either. Surely he didn't expect her to stay on with Sheena when he brought his new bride into the house. That would be asking too much.

She needed to think about her future. If she didn't marry Seth she would have to look for a job, and a flat or a bedsitter. She was determined not to go back to her old home.

Next day, while out riding with Seth, he brought up the subject of his proposal once again.

'Have you thought about what I said?' he demanded, reining in his horse and sliding to the ground.

They were on a bridle path through Huntsman's Wood, and birds were singing all around them. Jenny answered carefully, playing for time.

'I think we should get to know each

other a little better, Seth. Marriage is a big step and I want to make sure I'm doing the right thing.'

He looked at her, slapping his riding crop against his leg impatiently.

'Listen, Jenny, I can see you're a bit nervous, which is only natural as this is your first time around, and maybe you're expecting something different, a mad, passionate love affair. But I've been there, remember, and I know that sort of thing doesn't last. The excitement dies down and the relationship enters a new phase, mutual respect, loyalty, companionship. That's what I'm offering you, Jenny. I'll give you anything else you ask for, within reason. You'll want children of your own, I expect, and I want that, too. Now, what do you say?'

Something seemed to click inside Jenny's mind. She knew that it was time to stop living in the past, time to move on.

'Yes, please, I accept,' she said, and he threw his crop into the air with a whoop of delight.

She smiled at his exuberance. She would do her best to make him a good wife. Silently, in a secret place in her heart, a place which would never be open to Seth, she said goodbye to Jake.

9

'My, what a beautiful ring!' Mary Gladstone said enthusiastically as she admired the gold band set with tiny emeralds which Jenny, and Seth had come across in a tiny antique shop in the town. 'You are a dark horse, Jenny! Fancy you landing a famous writer for yourself. You will lead an interesting life, I'm sure. And when is the wedding to be?'

'We haven't decided yet, but Seth wants us to go to Venice in September, because he wants to do background research for a book, so we should think about it soon.'

'I should say so! There's a lot to do, planning a wedding. Invitations, dresses, bridesmaids, and of course you must see the vicar at once. And the cake! I'd better order the fruit and get that made, so it has time to mellow.'

'It won't be a big wedding,' Jenny said. 'Neither of us has many relations to ask, and this being the second time around for Seth, he doesn't want a big fuss.'

Mary grunted.

'That's all very well for him. It's your big day we're talking about. Everything should be as you want it. He should be pleased to follow on.'

'I agree with him, really. I'll have Rhonda for my bridesmaid, of course, and Seth means to ask his cousin, John, to be best man.'

'And we'll ask Mr Jake to give you away,' Mary said, and was utterly taken aback when Jenny shouted, 'No!'

There was a long silence.

'I'm sorry,' Jenny told her, in a trembling voice. 'You took me by surprise, saying that Jake could give me away. Dad will do that.'

'Of course! I'd quite forgotten that your father is still living,' Mary replied. 'You never talk about him, do you?'

But Jenny could see by her face that

the older woman was puzzled by her vehement response, and hastened to throw her off the scent.

'Dad has always been the quiet sort,' she began, 'and he's retreated into his shell since Ruth died. But of course he'd be thrilled to be a part of my wedding, and I couldn't think of asking anyone else to give me away.'

Mary looked at her with narrowed eyes.

'You can't pull the wool over my eyes, young woman. Of course your father comes first, but other than that there must be a very strong reason why you'd be so against your own brother-in-law giving you away. He's one of the family, too. Now, what's this all about? I know he's been rather remote ever since you arrived, in fact I'd say he's been downright rude at times, which isn't like him, but surely it hasn't been that bad?'

Jenny said nothing. There was another long pause and then, as understanding dawned, Mary slapped both hands down on the table, making Jenny jump.

'You're in love with Mr Jake! That's it! I'm right, aren't I?'

Jenny nodded slowly.

'Then why, in the name of goodness, have you got yourself engaged to another man?'

'I'm fond of Seth and Benjy, and I'd like to settle down and have a home and children of my own. I'm not doing anything wrong, Mary. Seth knows I'm not madly in love with him but he says mutual respect and companionship are more important in the long run.'

'That's as may be, but what about Mr Jake? Does he know how you feel about him?'

'I'm beginning to think he hates me, Mary.'

'Hates you? Such nonsense. Whatever makes you say such a thing?'

'It's as you said. He's practically ignored me ever since I arrived. You'd never think that he was the one who begged me to come here for Sheena's sake. And you should have seen the look he gave me when he saw me in the restaurant with Seth! No, Mary, I don't know what I've done to deserve this, but Jake hates me.'

'They do say that love and hate are not very far part,' Mary said, almost to herself, but there was a glint in her eye that said the subject was by no means closed.

The next step for Jenny was to break the news to her parents. All the way home on the bus she wondered what they would have to say, but she needn't have worried. Doris was delighted.

'I'm so pleased for you, Jenny. He'll have to come to tea so we can get to know him, and the little boy, too. Benjamin, is it?'

'Yes, but he's called Benjy. He's Sheena's age, Mum. In fact, that's how I met Seth, when we took the children to the play group in the village.'

A thought struck Doris.

'This Seth, he's not a divorced man, is he?'

'No, no, he's a widower. Bella died, from cancer, I understand, when Benjy was just a baby.'

Doris nodded.

'And I suppose he wants a wife to help him with the little boy. It was the same when your mother died. Your dad couldn't manage alone, so he married me. Well, we rub along all right and I daresay it will be the same with you two.'

Doris had never been one for cosy chats, but now she and her stepdaughter were on the same wavelength and she settled down with a large pot of tea in front of her, with an endless stream of questions on the tip of her tongue. What was his cottage like? Did he own it, or rent it? She was glad to hear that it was furnished with good, solid stuff, inherited from Seth's parents, not that utility stuff which was all there was to buy since the war.

'And the sister, Jessie, you say her name is? What does she do? Does she live with him? Could be trouble there, unless you can winkle her out.'

'No, she lives in London, Mum. She's just visiting at the moment. She seems very nice, though, down-to-earth and all that.'

The back door rattled.

'That'll be your dad, back from his allotment. Fred! Hurry up. Jenny's here and she's got something to tell us.'

'Got to get my boots off first, have a bit of a wash.'

'I'll make another pot while we're waiting, but get a move on, do!'

Doris couldn't wait to share the news. Her husband, tipping three lumps of sugar into his cup, was quietly pleased.

'Ah, well, time you settled down, old girl. And he's a writer, you say? Would I have read any of his stuff?'

This was just his way of showing an interest. As far as Fred was concerned, books were foreign territory. He took a daily paper because of the sports section and, as he said, why did you need to read the news when you could get the same thing on television? It was mostly all bad, anyhow.

Jenny told them about Seth's work, but Doris was more interested in the wedding arrangements.

'It's good of Mary to make the cake. I'm good with a sponge, as well you know, but fruit cakes have me beat. The fruit always sinks to the bottom, somehow. Thing is, where are we going to feed the guests? This place is too small and it costs money to hire a hall, and caterers.'

'There won't be many guests,' Jenny started to say, but Doris was already making a list on the back of an old envelope.

'Depends whether we invite children or not. If it's just adults, we could squeeze them in, I suppose, but then where are they all going to stay? Aunt May has to come all the way from Bournemouth and we can't put her up here, unless I tell Charlie she's got to find somewhere else to go for a couple of nights.'

Apparently this was the new lodger in Jenny's room.

'You'll be lucky.' Fred sniffed. 'You know what's she's like. Once she's in, you can't get her shifted.'

As they bickered amiably Jenny's mind began to wander, but she came back down to earth with a start when she heard her stepmother's triumphant cry.

'I've got it! The Old Mill House!'

'What?'

Jenny couldn't believe her ears.

'You could have the reception there. There's that lovely big room with the balcony in it, and all those bedrooms going to waste. Why not? If Ruth was alive she'd have wanted you to have it there, I know she would. It's the least Jake can do for you, after all these months you've looked after Sheena.'

'It's too far away, Mum. If I'm getting married at St Margaret's, how are the guests supposed to get to the Old Mill House? It's miles away, and none of them has cars.'

'Imagine them lined up at the bus stop, all dressed up,' Fred chortled, but Doris had it all worked out.

'No reason it has to be St Margaret's, just because the bride usually gets married in her own local church. I'm sure they have churches close by. Most of the guests will have to travel from home anyway, so they may as well go there as come here. Your dad and I can come over the day before and we'll be on the spot in good time.'

'I don't think so, Mum,' Jenny said weakly, but Doris was not to be deterred.

'I'll go over to Mrs Foster's later and give Jake a ring. She never minds me using her phone so long as I put the coppers in the Dr Barnardo's box. Then, if Jake says yes, I should try to get over to the house in the near future and have a word with Mary Gladstone. If she's as good a cook as you say, she may be willing to do the catering if we slip her a bit on the side.'

Jenny felt slightly sick. How had

things got out of hand so fast? Still, she had lived with Doris long enough to know that any protest would be futile. Get on the wrong side of her stepmother and she'd never hear the last of it. Her best plan would be to have a quiet word with Seth. Perhaps he wouldn't mind a register office wedding with just a handful of their nearest and dearest in attendance.

10

Doris lived up to her word and phoned Jake. The first Jenny knew of this was when Mary Gladstone called her into the kitchen. After settling Sheena at the table with a handful of currants and raisins she looked Jenny straight in the eye and said, 'So you plan to go through with this farce.'

'I don't know what you mean,' Jenny countered, on the defensive.

'I think you do. We've had your stepmother on the phone, wanting Mr Jake to host your wedding reception here.'

'Oh.'

'Don't you 'oh' me, my girl. You may be Mr Jake's sister-in-law and myself only the hired hand, but the time has come for some plain speaking. It's my belief you're in love with Jake, and that being the case it's downright folly to hook yourself up to some other man. Not fair to that Mr Wilcox, either. Oh, you may think now that you can make him a good wife, but sooner or later it will come to grief, you mark my words. Now, am I right, or am I not?'

Jenny began to cry, the tears seeping from under her closed eyelids. At that moment Mrs Hopper happened to come into the kitchen, making her way through to the garden. Mary gesticulated at Sheena and then at Jenny, and the housekeeper got the message.

'Would you like to come out and help Hoppy pick some flowers for the house, dear?' Miss Hopper asked.

Sheena nodded vigorously and, hastily cramming the last raisins into her mouth, followed the woman outside.

'There now,' Mary said, 'we can speak freely, so let's hurry up and get to the bottom of this before they come back.'

Dabbing at her eyes with her sodden handkerchief, Jenny took a deep breath and began. It would be a relief to unburden herself to somebody who knew Jake really well.

'You're right, Mary. I've been in love with Jake for a long time. I don't know if you're aware of this, but we'd been going out together for several months before he ever met Ruth, and I thought the feeling was mutual. There was no engagement or anything like that. There was no hurry, of course, but I hoped that perhaps our relationship would lead to marriage in the end.'

'And then he met your sister?'

'Yes, Ruth came home from college and I had to introduce them. I was a bit worried at first because she had a habit of taking my boyfriends away from me. It was all a big joke to her. She was so much prettier than I was, and so witty and lively, I never stood a chance against her.'

'I see, and so it happened again, and she stole Mr Jake from you?'

'Well, no, that was the funny thing in all this. She was very sweet, and told me she could see I was really in love, and she was glad for me. She didn't set out to charm him, or act flirtatiously. She didn't even stay around when he came to the house, although they often saw each other at dances and tennis parties, things like that.'

The kitchen clock ticked on loudly while Mary digested this.

'Then how did it come about that Mr Jake married your sister? He must have felt a bit awkward, marrying her when he'd been courting you, for that's how I see it. How did he explain himself to you?'

'That's just it. He didn't.'

'Surely he must have said something? He owed you that much.'

Jenny shook her head.

'That's what hurt so much. He simply stopped coming to see me. I tried phoning him, but he was never available. I wrote letters, but never received a reply. Then Ruth came home one day and said they were engaged.'

'You should have demanded an explanation, my dear.'

'He'd made it plain that he wanted nothing to do with me. I do have some pride, you know. It broke my heart, Mary, but what was the point of talking about it if he didn't love me?'

For once Mary seemed lost for words, as Jenny went on.

'I've been a fool, Mary. Nobody knows this except my friend, Rhonda, but when Jake sent me that pleading letter, asking me to come and look after Sheena, I hoped that he'd turn to me again. Rhonda warned me that I was just setting myself up for more misery, and she was right. He hasn't given me the time of day and now he's flaunting that Magda Hall under my nose. So I've finally come to my senses. It's time to move on, Mary, and if Seth wants me, I'll accept his proposal and be glad of the chance.'

Mary said no more, but her mind was in a whirl. She flattered herself that she knew Jake as well as any living soul, with the possible exception of his parents, and this story didn't ring true.

Not that she doubted Jenny by any means, but she did not believe that Jake could have acted in such a cowardly way. From being a courageous, small boy he had grown into a man of integrity. Surely he would have faced up to his mistake, admitting honestly to Jenny that he had fallen for her sister.

In Mary's opinion, some men were not very wise when it came to understanding women, and if he was planning to marry the Hall woman that proved it! Jake was like a son to Mary, and she was determined to get to the bottom of this. She was aware that Jenny would not wish her to interfere, so wisely she said nothing to her. She knew she had to act quickly. Seth was pressuring Jenny to marry him as soon as possible, and with Magda Hall waiting in the wings Jake was in danger of making another mistake.

Meanwhile, Rhonda's friend, the librarian, Peter Steele, had approached Seth to give a reading at the library. At least, he had spoken to Jenny, asking rather diffidently if she thought that Seth would do it.

'We don't have much in the way of funds so we could only pay expenses, but it would be a big drawing card for the Friends of the Library annual meeting if he would consider coming. We just can't keep his books on the shelves and there is always a waiting list for any new title. I had no idea he lived in the area until Rhonda mentioned it.'

'I'll certainly put it to him,' Jenny responded, 'and perhaps the four of us could go out for a meal together before the event.'

She had taken a liking to the gangly red-headed man and was eager to further Rhonda's cause. He agreed to her suggestion at once, but Seth was less enthusiastic.

'I hate these affairs,' he moaned. 'You put everything on one side to attend one of the things and about three people show up. The organisers get into a flap, trying to come up with excuses for the poor attendance. It must be the rain. It must be the fine weather. It must be the boxing match on television.'

'Please, Seth. I really hoped you'd do it. It would mean so much to Rhonda.'

'Then we mustn't let Rhonda down,' he said, raising his eyebrows. 'But a reading is out. My sort of stuff doesn't lend itself to that. How do you pick a few pages out of a fast-paced thriller, when the audience doesn't know what went before, or how the story will end?'

Jenny could see his point.

'I'll give them a talk on a day in the life of a writer, that sort of thing. Will that do?'

She agreed that it would.

Jenny dipped into her dwindling savings to buy a lovely new dress and shoes for the occasion.

'You look very smart,' Mary Gladstone remarked. 'Turquoise goes well with your dark hair. Do you have a hat and gloves to go with that lot?'

'No, it's not that dressy an occasion,' Jenny told her. 'Just as well, really. I've hardly anything left in my savings account.'

She said this ruefully and Mary's mouth tightened. That poor girl. It sounded as if Jake hadn't given her a penny piece all these months. He must have known she wouldn't have any money coming in, having given up her job to come here. Well, that put the tin lid on it, she decided. She'd been wrestling with her conscience, wondering if she ought to interfere and now her mind was made up.

Seth's talk was a great success. The boardroom of the library was filled to bursting and extra chairs had to be brought in from the school next door. Jenny had never seen Seth in action before and was impressed by his smooth delivery and his ability to keep the audience enthralled. After the presentation the questions came thick and fast. Had the books been translated into any other languages? Had he ever won any awards? Were any of the characters based on real people?

Seth explained that all his characters were fictional, but if one of them happened to bear a striking resemblance to a rather sinister-looking master at his old school, well, it must have been his subconscious mind at work. Everyone laughed, and Jenny felt a glow of pride.

With Jenny out of the house that evening, Mary steeled herself to tackle Jake. She knew that he was planning to work at home that night so it was the perfect opportunity. Hanging up her apron on the hook behind the kitchen door, she gave her hands a quick wash before glancing in the mirror to make sure that no strands of hair had escaped from her grey bun. Then she went into battle.

Passing the door of what had been Ruth's sitting-room she was surprised to hear voices coming from inside. The door flew open and Sheena rushed out.

'I don't like that lady!' she shouted, and promptly burst into tears.

Magda Hall followed her out, her

face flushed with anger.

'And if you were mine you'd get a good smacking!' she snapped. 'Just look at what the little brat did to my new lipstick! Where's her nanny, anyway? She's not much good if she can't keep her eye on the child for five minutes!'

The tube had been pushed open to the fullest extent and only a trace of the contents remained. The child reeked of perfume, so she had probably rifled Magda's handbag, opening a bottle of scent as well.

'What on earth is going on here?' Jake asked, alerted by the raised voices, and emerging from his study, looking grim.

Taking in the scene at a glance he took Magda by the elbow and steered her back into the room.

'I'll sort this out, Magda. I'll see you later.'

He closed the door behind her. Sheena hurled herself on her protector, sobbing wildly. Her little hands clutched at Mary's skirts, leaving vivid crimson streaks on the starched cotton. Mary hurried her into the nearby toilet to sponge her off. Jake followed, lounging in the doorway.

'You mustn't touch Miss Hall's things, sweetheart, she doesn't like it,' he said to his daughter.

Sheena stamped her foot.

'I don't like the nasty lady, Daddy. I don't want her to be in my mummy's room.'

'And speaking of which, why is Miss Hall in there?' Mary wanted to know. 'I wasn't aware she was here at all, or I'd have kept a closer eye on her, with Jenny out for the evening.'

Jake patted his daughter on her dungareed bottom, telling her to run along and play.

'I was going to tell you, Gladdie. I just haven't had a chance yet. As it seems that Jenny will soon be leaving us to get married, I've decided I should spend more time with Sheena. I'm taking a leaf out of that Wilcox fellow's book and doing some work here at home. I really don't need to be in the office every day of the week.'

Mary nodded, glad to see Jake taking more of an interest in his little girl. That was all to the good, surely?

'And what about that Miss Hall? Where does she fit into all this?'

'She has a little car, so she'll be reporting here for work on the days when I'm in session. Ruth's room seems like the ideal spot for her. I'm having a few things brought in, a filing cabinet and a typewriter, but we'll have to tidy up in there first, which is why Magda is here this evening. I thought that Jenny might like to take some of her sister's things to her new home.'

'Very thoughtful of you, I'm sure,' Mary said drily. 'Could we go to your study, Mr Jake? There's something I'd like to say to you, in private.'

But at that moment the door to the sitting-room opened again and Magda stuck her head out.

'I'd like a cup of coffee, please, cook, black, with two lumps of sugar,' she said and disappeared again.

Cook, indeed! Mary glared at Jake but his face was impassive. The moment had passed. What she had to say would have to wait.

'I'll get that coffee,' she snapped, and turned to go.

'I'll have one as well, please, while you're at it,' Jake murmured, 'and isn't it time Sheena was in bed? I thought she seemed over-tired.'

So nothing more was said.

11

Jenny had never seen a man pout before, but if Seth wasn't serious he was certainly putting on a good act.

'I know that this is your wedding, Jenny, and the bride's family makes most of the decisions concerning the arrangements, but I simply cannot understand why you are acting like this. I mean, if you don't want a church wedding, I'll go along with that. I don't have strong feelings one way or the other. But the reception! Why try to cram everyone into your parents' little place when Jake has generously offered to let you have the use of the Old Mill House?'

'I've told you. It wasn't my idea. It was Mum.'

'I'm sure that if your sister had been alive she'd have insisted on it.'

'Well, she's not alive, is she?'

Jenny was aware that she was being difficult but she could hardly explain her reasons to Seth. In any case he was in full flow and not prepared to listen.

'I don't think you quite understand my position, Jenny. Though I say it myself I'm quite well known and we simply cannot just slope off and make our wedding a hole-in-the-corner affair. The Press will be out in full force and there are sure to be photos in the newspapers, that sort of thing. I'm not saying anything against your old home. It's a very pleasant house of its kind. It's just that the Old Mill House would be better for my image.'

Annoyed, Jenny pushed down the indignant retort that rose to her lips. This was her wedding day, and he was thinking about his image! And if such things were so important to him, why was he living at Rose Cottage, instead of buying an Old Mill House for himself? Then she chided herself for being stupid. Jake had inherited the estate. She had no idea of land values but probably no ordinary person could afford to buy such a place nowadays. She didn't know how much money Seth made from his international bestsellers but with taxation being as high it was, he was probably not in that league.

'And I haven't even seen the inside of that house,' Seth went on, a petulant note creeping into his voice. 'If I didn't know better, I'd almost think that you didn't want me to meet your sainted brother-in-law. But perhaps it's his fault, not yours. The least he could have done was to throw an engagement dinner for us, after all you've done for his little girl.'

Jenny said nothing, and Seth went on.

'We'll have to see something of each other in the future, you know. After all, Benjy and Sheena will be cousins soon.'

Jenny hadn't thought of that. As Sheena's aunt, and soon to be Benjy's stepmother, she would be the tie between them. And Sheena had come to depend on her. She couldn't simply fade into the background and never see the child again, especially if she was soon to be left to the not-so-tender mercies of Magda Hall! Why did life have to be so complicated?

Doris entered into the wedding preparations with gusto. Trying to pluck up the courage to tell her stepmother that the reception would not be held at the Old Mill House, Jenny allowed herself to be swept into a spate of shopping and chatter.

'We must look for the perfect wedding dress,' Doris enthused. 'We'll go to Benson's first. They have a bridal department, don't they?'

'Yes, that's right.'

On many occasions she and Rhonda had wandered into the bridal department in their lunch hour, dreamily assessing the relative merits of the gowns on display. Jenny had imagined herself finding the perfect dress there for her wedding to Jake, but that had been long ago, before all her dreams were shattered.

To prepare themselves for the fray, Doris steered Jenny up to the restaurant on the top floor, where they ordered tea and cream cakes. It soon became evident that it wasn't the tea Doris wanted so much as the opportunity to show off to all her cronies.

'You remember my daughter, Jenny? We're here to shop for her wedding dress. She's going to marry Seth Wilcox, the author, you know?'

'And is the wedding to be at St Margaret's?' one woman asked.

Jenny excused herself, saying that she wanted to slip downstairs to see if Rhonda was about. She knew it was her friend's day off, but she had to get away. Poor Doris was a bit of a snob but perhaps she couldn't be blamed for that. Her life seldom held any excitement and she had been a bit depressed since Ruth's death. Jenny dreaded having to burst her bubble.

★ ★ ★

Mary Gladstone was pleased when Jake came into her kitchen.

'Any fresh Eccles cakes, Gladdie?' he asked.

'You must have smelled them baking! Here you are. Mind you don't burn your mouth.'

He sat down at the table, licking the crumbs off his fingers. Mary seized her chance.

'Jenny's gone shopping, with her mother.'

'Oh?'

'For her wedding outfit,' she said meaningly. 'Although how she's supposed to pay for anything, I don't know.'

'What do you mean?'

'Money, Mr Jake. I don't know if it's occurred to you, but since she's come here she hasn't been making a penny piece.'

He frowned, and having taken the plunge she went on bravely.

'She gave up her job when you asked her to come here to look after little

Sheena, and that was months ago. I know for a fact she's used up all her savings, not that she's complained to me, mind. Why are you treating her like this, Mr Jake? It's not like you to be selfish. I know she has her meals and a roof over her head, but if you brought in a professional nanny you'd have to give her a proper wage as well, so why not Jenny?'

He reached for another pastry.

'You don't know what you're talking about, Gladdie. I told her to charge things to my account at Parker & Johnson's.'

'Men! That was all very well for Sheena's bits and pieces, but do you think any decent girl would do that for herself? Make her feel like a kept woman, that would. No, she should be given a proper wage, then she needn't feel beholden. I daresay that Miss Hall gets paid, doesn't she?'

'That's entirely different.'

'No, it is not,' Mary said.

Standing upright with her arms

folded she looked the picture of outrage, and Jake had to laugh.

'I suppose you're right. I didn't give it a thought. I'll give her a decent cheque for a wedding present. How's that?'

'I suppose that will have to do. But, Mr Jake, there's something else I want to talk to you about.'

'Can't it wait? I have a mound of paperwork on my desk, and I have to make a call to Germany before noon. Thanks for the cakes. Wonderful, as usual. I don't know how I'd ever exist without you, Mary.'

Patting her on her rosy cheek he loped from the room, leaving her not knowing whether to laugh or to cry.

★ ★ ★

Jenny's mind was in a turmoil. She needed to get away by herself to think. She went to the stables and hired her favourite little chestnut mare, Poppy, and rode off through Huntsman's

Wood, emerging at the other side to climb the hill to the lookout point where she could see the valley spread out below. Once there she kicked her feet out of the stirrups and slid to the ground, leaving her horse to graze contentedly.

Things were getting out of hand. Jenny had come to realise that her troubles were partly of her own making. If she wrote to an agony aunt at a magazine she would no doubt be told that she was too timid, and needed to take charge of her life.

When Ruth and Jake had announced their engagement, leaving her shocked and bewildered, she should have insisted on an explanation. Instead, she had crawled away to lick her wounds in private, actually seeing Jake's point of view, believing that he had innocently discovered that his love for Ruth was greater than his attachment to Jenny. Had the shoe been on the other foot, Ruth would not have taken this lying down!

Then, when Jake had crooked his little finger, she had actually come running, ignoring everyone's advice, just like a spurned puppy crawling to the master who had punished it. At that moment, Jenny despised herself.

'It's not too late to change,' she told Poppy, who, not surprisingly, made no response, but went on chomping.

The first thing to do was to break off her engagement to Seth. He might be satisfied with the limitations of their relationship but Mary Gladstone was right. Neither of them should settle for second best. Then she would have to break the news to her parents, which wouldn't be pleasant. Dad would understand, but Doris would be indignant, losing face with the neighbours after all her boasting. But that would have to be faced, and after that, Jenny intended to move away, leaving the past behind her. Where she would go and what she could do she didn't yet know, but she was young and healthy, and would come up with something.

Perhaps she could get a job as a mother's help. Surely Jake would provide her with a good reference, or she might even enter nurse training and try to do some good in the world.

Later that day she cycled over to Rose Cottage, meaning to tell Seth her decision. Leaning her bike against the fence she let herself in by the back door, and then came to a halt as she heard her name mentioned.

'Jenny won't mind, will she?'

That was Jessie speaking. It was wrong to listen, of course, and the old, spineless Jenny might have crept away, but now she wanted to know what new decisions were being made on her behalf.

'Oh, I shouldn't think so,' Seth said easily. 'You like each other, don't you?'

'Well, yes, she's a nice enough girl. It's just that things have never been the same at the office since the war, with all the men coming back to civvy street. Now, after all the responsibilities we took on back then, we women are second class citizens again. I've a nice little nest egg put by so I could easily retire, and think how useful I could be here. I could look after young Benjamin, leaving Jenny free to go with you on these research outings you're always talking about, and if other children come along in time, an extra pair of hands in the house would always be useful.'

'The only thing is, old girl, the lack of accommodation. Three bedrooms would do us for now, but if our family increases . . . '

'I've thought of that,' Jessie said, her voice sounding triumphant. 'I'll sell my little house in London. I should get a good price for it now, and put the money into enlarging this place. We could build an extension out into the shrubbery and knock a door through from the end of the hall. It would be perfect. Come on, I'll show you what I mean, and if you agree, maybe we could get the builders in when you're away in Venice, so you'd miss all the upheaval.'

Jenny tiptoed back outside. She was sure they hadn't heard her come in. She would wait a while and then ring her bicycle bell and call out to them, as if just arriving. Thank goodness she had heard all this before speaking to Seth. If she had broken off their engagement after being presented with a fait accompli he would have thought it had something to do with her not wanting Jessie on the premises. She suspected that he would either get upset, because he was very fond of his older sister, or he would offer to make the sacrifice of turning Jessie down, and then she would have even more trouble convincing him that marriage wasn't on the cards.

Taking a deep breath, she re-entered the house. Seth greeted her with a smile.

'There you are, Jenny. I'm glad you've come. Jessie has had a splendid idea. Come on through to the back hall and we'll show you what we've decided to do.'

'Not now, Seth. Do you mind if we talk in private?' she asked, as Jessie joined them, her eyes sparkling.

'Yes, it's best you discuss this by yourselves,' Jessie said. 'I'll go down the garden and see what Benjy is up to. He's in his play-house, I expect.'

The door closed behind her. It wasn't like her to be so tactful, but of course she didn't want anything to spoil her plan. Jenny gulped, and came straight to the point.

'I'm so very sorry, Seth, but I can't marry you. I just can't.'

'Pre-wedding jitters!' He laughed. 'Every bride has them. I remember Margaret, my first wife . . . '

She interrupted him, not an easy task when Seth was in full flow.

'It's not nerves, Seth. I've tried to explain before that I'm not in love with you, and you say it doesn't matter, but I believe it does. It wouldn't be fair to you or to Benjy if I couldn't put my whole heart into this marriage.'

He swept her into his arms, obviously

hoping to kiss her doubts away, but she struggled free.

'It's no good, Seth. I'm greatly honoured that you've asked me to be your wife, and I've considered everything very carefully, but my mind is made up. I know now that I shouldn't have agreed to an engagement in the first place, but surely it's better to end it now than to get married and have it fall apart later.'

'This is going to make me look a fool,' he muttered. 'I just hope the Press doesn't get hold of this, that's all.'

Jenny knew then that she had made the right decision. If Seth had said something about being in love with her, not knowing how he could go on without her, she might have wavered, but all he was worried about was his precious image! He had a right to be annoyed, of course, even disappointed, but a wife was a bit more than a mere possession!

Probably he wanted a wife to provide him with home comforts, to look after him and his little boy while he got on with his precious writing! Well then, she was no loss. He had Jessie waiting in the wings, and with the bride missing from the picture they wouldn't even have to build an addition on the house.

Seth said some rather unkind things and Jenny let him ramble on. She felt guilty about turning him down and probably did deserve them, she told herself.

'Well, if that's your final answer, I suppose there's no more to be said,' he remarked at last.

Jenny pulled off her ring and placed it in his outstretched hand. Then head bowed, she walked out of the house, without looking back.

12

As she had expected, Jenny had to undergo a grilling from Doris. Foolish, unreliable and ungrateful were just a few of the names hurled at her by her disappointed stepmother. Gran was the only one who seemed to understand. She listened to Jenny's explanation and then spoke quietly.

'You know best, dear. In my book, marriage is for life and you can't enter into it lightly, or to please other people. Doris will get over it, and from what you say, that Seth doesn't sound too devastated. As you say, I expect he only wants someone to look after him and the little boy while he gets on with his writing. Don't you fret, dear. Mr Right will come along sooner or later. Like the song says, whatever will be, will be.'

Feeling despondent, Jenny stayed away from places where she was likely to run into Seth, including the play group and the stables, so she had to make other arrangements to make sure that Sheena didn't suffer. Several of the mothers were quite willing to bring their children to play at the Old Mill House and extended invitations to Sheena in return.

They all seemed keen to have a peek inside the house, and for her part Jenny was glad to share coffee and conversation with other women who knew nothing of her personal problems.

One evening, she and Sheena had finished having their tea in the nursery and Jenny had given her niece a bath and put her to bed. The child lay there contentedly, tucked up with her family of battered teddy bears. Jenny opened the dumb waiter and was about to place the tray of crockery inside when she heard voices, wafting up the shaft from the kitchen below — Jake and Mary Gladstone. She could hear quite clearly what was being said, and they were talking about her.

151

'This is becoming a habit,' she told herself guiltily, but she could no more have closed the hatch than she could have flown in the air.

'I've watched what's been going on here,' Mary was saying, 'and I must say I don't understand what it's all about. I thought I knew you better than that, Mr Jake.'

'Come off it, Gladdie. I told you I was sorry, and planned to give her a decent wedding present to make up for forgetting about wages.'

'I'm not talking about that. I want to know why you've treated her like a leper ever since she got here. When have you even sat down to dinner with her, or offered to take her out for a meal?'

Jake muttered something that Jenny couldn't catch and then she heard him clear his throat and begin again.

'I'm going to tell you something, Gladdie, something I've never told a living soul, and if you dare to repeat it to anyone, especially Jenny, I'll pack you off to that sister of yours before you can say boo.'

'Well, go on.'

'I knew Jenny before I met Ruth, in fact we went out together for several months.'

'Jenny has mentioned that.'

'And did she happen to mention that I fell in love with her and asked her to marry me?'

Two floors above, Jenny's heart began to thump painfully. He had never asked her any such thing!

'No, she didn't tell me that,' Mary said.

'No, I don't suppose she did. I thought we were on the same wavelength but suddenly she broke off with me, with no warning and no explanation. I tried to find out what had gone wrong, don't think I didn't, but she refused to see me and returned my letters, unopened. I was cut to the quick, Gladdie, I didn't know which way to turn.'

'But obviously you did, for you

married her sister.'

Mary seemed puzzled by the way the story was unfolding.

'Ruth was so sweet to me while all this was going on. She thought it was terrible that Jenny would treat me like that. She told me she'd tried to talk to her about it, but Jenny just told her to go away and leave her alone. I felt like retreating from the world for a while, but Ruth coaxed me along and gradually I began to want to face living again. All I wanted was peace, and Ruth was so feminine and loving, I felt I could do worse than settle down with her. I suppose I married her on the rebound, and you know the rest.'

'And then you make the mistake of asking Jenny to come here to look after Sheena, and seeing her here brought it all back.'

'That's right. After more than four years I believed I was over her, but life is never that easy, is it, Gladdie? And coming face to face with her every day has made me angry, remembering how

I'd been tricked.'

Jenny was furious. How dare he say such wicked things? Without stopping to think, she hurtled downstairs, her feet barely touching the steps. She yanked the kitchen door open, greeted by two startled faces.

'How dare you talk about me like that, Jake Thomas-Harding! I knew you were a rotten beast, but I didn't realise you were a liar, too! I want an explanation right now, and I refuse to take no for an answer!'

'I'd better go up and listen for Sheena,' Mary said, sliding out of the door, but neither Jake nor Jenny heard her go.

For a long moment they glared at each other and then Jake sighed wearily and said he supposed they'd better sit down.

'I heard everything you said about me,' Jenny snapped, sliding into a chair, 'and I don't know how you had the nerve to come out with such rubbish.'

'Listeners never hear good of themselves,' he sneered. 'I never thought you'd sink to eavesdropping, Jenny, and that's a fact.'

'I didn't mean to! I was just putting the tea things on the dumb waiter and the sound travelled up the shaft. When I heard you telling Mary all those lies I had to find out what was happening.'

He took her by the wrist, a pleading look on his face, but she jerked her hand away. Angry tears spilled from her eyes.

'Don't you touch me, Jake! I'm waiting for an explanation. What you've done to me in the past is one thing, but it's nothing compared with what went on here this evening. Making out that I was the one who broke it off, refusing to discuss it, when actually it was you, yourself, who behaved that way. I suppose you thought Mary would believe you and turn against me, when you've been together so long. Well, it doesn't matter much either way, because I shan't be here much longer.

Then I hope I'll never see you again.'

'Fat chance of that, when you'll be the famous Mrs Wilcox, living on the other side of the village,' he said, curling his lip.

'For your information, the wedding's off. And, despite what you may think of me, I didn't run and hide when I realised I'd made a mistake. I faced Seth honestly, even though it was not very pleasant. I wasn't a coward, like you were when you broke my heart.'

'Oh, Jenny,' Jake said wearily, rubbing his eyes with his knuckles, looking so much like Sheena when she was overtired that Jenny felt a pang of love and pity. 'If you hadn't come tearing downstairs when you did you might have heard the rest of the story. Are you prepared to listen to it now?'

What did she have to lose? They couldn't leave matters like this. She nodded slowly. This had to be played out to the bitter end.

'It all had to do with Ruth,' he began. 'I know it's not the thing to speak ill of the dead, but it can't be helped. It started when I had to make a quick trip to Paris, on business. I knew you'd never been there and thought you might like to go along. Your parents aren't on the phone, of course, so I sent a messenger round with a note, asking for you to call me when you got home from work, to make arrangements.'

Jenny frowned.

'Paris! Are you sure, Jake? I mean, maybe the message went to the wrong address, or Mum was out, or something.'

He shook his head.

'I received a phone call, all right, but it was from Ruth. You couldn't get the day off work, she told me, but she was free and would love to see Paris. I was a bit uncomfortable with it, but she said it was fine with you, so off we went. Nothing happened, Jenny, I swear! I left her looking round the Louvre while I dashed off to my meeting, and after that we did a few of the touristy things, like having a drink in an outdoor cafe, and going to see the Eiffel Tower, and then we started back for the ferry.'

Jenny stared at him, wide-eyed.

'Ruth said nothing to me about any trip to Paris, I know she didn't.'

'So it would seem. After that I lost contact with you. I sent letters and they came back unopened. I called at the house, but you were never there, or, if you were, you made Ruth answer the door and send me away. Through it all, she was sweet and loving. You were furious because I'd taken her to Paris instead of you, she told me. You felt that I had betrayed you and you wanted nothing more to do with a man you couldn't trust.'

Jenny felt really sick. It wasn't Jake who had betrayed her, it had been her own sister.

'But if you really cared you should have insisted on speaking to me, Jake. You knew my working hours, you knew where I lived.'

'As I told you, I did try, of course I did, but your stepmother insisted that you were too angry to talk to me and she thought it was best if I went away and left you alone.'

Doris! Had Ruth pulled the wool over her eyes, too, or was it possible that she had been part of this, wanting her own daughter to marry the wealthy Jake Thomas-Harding and become mistress of the Old Mill House? Surely not! It was too much like the story of Cinderella, except that in this case there had been no glass slipper for Prince Charming to place on Jenny's foot.

She pushed that thought away. Doris was far from being the wicked step-mother. While she might want to see her daughter well settled, she had always treated Jenny with kindness and would not have connived to spoil her happiness. Nor would she have been so cruel as to force Jenny to be bridesmaid when Ruth and Jake were married if she had believed that she harboured feelings for the man. Thinking back, she was sure that she had never told Doris about those feelings. She had confided in Ruth, of course, and her friend Rhonda, but had said little to her parents beyond the fact that she and Jake were dating.

'I'm sorry, Jake. All of this is news to me, but I can well believe it. This was another of Ruth's schemes, of course.'

'I'm aware of that now,' he told her, 'but there are things you don't know yet. All through our marriage Ruth behaved flirtatiously with other men. I believed it was harmless, just her manner. You know how she was, always witty and full of life. A few months after Sheena was born I caught her in another man's arms. We had gone to a party and when I stepped out on the terrace to get a breath of air, there was Ruth in the moonlight, kissing Tom Robinson, a friend of ours. She swore it meant nothing and said it would never happen again, but of course it did, this time with one of my business associates, here in our own home. We had a monumental row and unforgivable things were said in the heat of the moment, things which should have been left unsaid.'

'Understandable, wasn't it?'

Jenny wasn't sure she wanted to hear intimate details of their married life, but he kept talking, staring into the distance as if seeing ghosts.

'I'm afraid I said something to the effect that Jenny might have let me down badly but at least she was loyal. I was convinced that you would never have turned to other men.'

'Oh, Jake!'

'Ruth laughed hysterically and taunted me about my precious Jenny! She said I should have married you instead of her and so I would have done if she hadn't put a spoke in my wheel. I asked her what she meant and she flung it at me, how she had so cleverly tricked the pair of us. So there you are, Jenny, that's my story. Two ruined lives. The only good thing to come out of this mess is Sheena.'

Jenny sat unmoving. She was filled with pain to think how they had both been duped. Anger at Ruth filled her heart. Ruth had gaily planned her wedding, knowing all the time how much her half sister must be hurting, to say nothing of her bridegroom. She remembered pouring her heart out to Jake in a letter, pleading with him to meet her one last time, to discuss this face to face. She remembered Ruth, trying to console her, offering to run down to the pillar box to post the letter so that Jenny wouldn't have to show her tear-blotched face in public.

There was no need to ask Jake if he had ever seen that letter. Ruth had destroyed it, of course. But now, what was the point of staying angry with Ruth? She was dead and gone. The horror receded as the truth began to sink in. Jake had not abandoned her, and he still had feelings for her. She reached across the table and took his clasped hands between her own.

'I'm glad you've told me all this, Jake. It must have been so painful for you, but I understand better now.'

She swallowed hard and went on.

'I've never stopped loving you, Jake. Even when I thought you'd treated me so badly, nothing could alter that.'

His eyes met hers again and his grim expression softened for a moment.

'So, when you invited me here,' she went on, 'I hoped you might feel something for me after all.'

'I did. That is, I do.'

Her heart soared.

'Then it's not too late for us, is it? We can't wipe out the past few years, but we can begin again.'

He was silent for a moment and then he muttered, 'There's no future for us, Jenny. I wish we could turn back the clock, but we can't.'

She was bewildered.

'But if we take things slowly.'

He shook his head.

'You still don't understand. When Ruth and I had that row, I shouted at her and told her to get out, out of the house and out of my life. She responded by packing a case and grabbing up Sheena and running out of the house. She was going to her parents, she told me, and I'd be hearing from her solicitor. That was the night she died, Jenny. She drove out of here in a fury and got involved in the accident which killed her. It was only by a miracle that Sheena survived. If I hadn't let them go that night Ruth would still be alive. I can never forgive myself for that and that's why we can never come together, Jenny. Too much water has passed under the bridge.'

13

While she could understand Jake's feelings, the new Jenny was not about to give up without a struggle. Until now she had let herself be swept along by events but when the next day dawned she felt refreshed and ready for action.

Her first port of call was to see Mary Gladstone. Mary greeted her in the kitchen with a wary expression on her face, and Jenny was determined to set the record straight.

'Jake and I had a long talk last evening, Mary. I suppose he hasn't said anything to you since I came down and disturbed you both.'

'No, he hasn't, and I don't think I ought to hear this. Whatever all the fuss was about is between the two of you. None of my business, is it? I don't want to be involved.'

'Please, let me explain, Mary. Believe me, I'm not trying to say anything against Jake. It's all been a huge misunderstanding from start to finish. We were in love, but my sister played us off against each other. She lied to us, and made each of us believe that we'd been deserted by the other. Then she stepped in and claimed Jake for herself.'

'More fool him, then,' Mary said stoutly, and Jenny giggled.

'I couldn't agree more, but that's hindsight. Ruth could be very convincing when she liked and we were completely taken in.'

'So that's what Mr Jake meant when he said he'd been tricked,' Mary mused. 'So what comes next then?'

Jenny shrugged. She decided not to mention what Jake had told her about Ruth rushing off to her death after their argument. If Jake wanted Mary Gladstone to know, he could tell her himself.

That weekend, on the Saturday, Jenny deposited Sheena at a little playmate's birthday party. The child had more confidence now and she waved gaily as she went to join the other children in the large, flower-filled garden, clutching a colourfully-wrapped gift. Jake had agreed to collect his daughter when the festivities were over, leaving Jenny free to catch the bus to see Rhonda.

Mrs Maxwell opened the door to her and immediately began to sing Seth's praises, congratulating her on his wonderful talk at the library.

'My husband was quite delighted and was only sorry he hadn't taken all his books along, to get them autographed. Now that Rhonda is seeing so much of Peter Steele, perhaps we could all get together some evening. Would you and Mr Wilcox like to come round for a meal?'

'I'm sorry, Mrs Maxwell, I'm afraid that won't be possible. Seth and I aren't seeing each other any more.'

'You don't mean to say you've broken off your engagement? Or has the wretched man jilted you? What a disaster! Isn't there any hope of a reconciliation? Perhaps it's just a lovers' tiff.'

Jenny was saved from answering by the appearance of Rhonda, who took her friend upstairs.

'You'll have to excuse Mum. She was so upset for me when Johnny jilted me and I suppose she doesn't want to see the same thing happening to you. Now, tell me all! You've really kicked Seth Wilcox into touch?'

Having heard the story she nodded approvingly.

'As you know, I always did think you were doing the wrong thing there. Besides, he's much too old for you, really.'

'That's right, say I told you so!'

Rhonda grinned at her friend affectionately.

'What I want to know is, where do you go from here? Can you stay on at the Old Mill House, or is the dreaded Magda still on the scene?'

She listened, wide-eyed, as Jenny went on to give details of her encounter with Jake.

'So you mean to tell me it was that little beast, Ruth, who was behind it all the time? I'm sorry, Jenny, I know she was your sister and all that but honestly, what a way to behave.'

'Anyway, it's all resolved between me and Jake now,' Jenny said. 'It's a relief to know that he wasn't such a rotter after all.'

'So is there a chance you'll get back together, live happily ever after?'

'I know that Jake still loves me,' Jenny told her, 'but right now he still feels responsible for Ruth's death. I have to give him time.'

'Then don't leave it too long. You lost him once before by being too timid. Do you want that Magda to get her hooks into him? You love Jake, so fight for him!'

★   ★   ★

Hearing sounds of furniture being moved inside Ruth's old sitting-room, Jenny knocked and went in. A typewriter was perched on top of a three-drawer filing cabinet and Magda was in the act of moving a beautiful, little gate-legged table closer to the window.

'Here, you can help me with this,' she ordered. 'I prefer to work with my back to the light, so this table will do nicely. That is, unless you're taking it away with you.'

'No, I'm not removing anything,' Jenny said pleasantly, 'but I hope you're going to put a cloth or something underneath the typewriter so the surface of that table doesn't get scratched. It's quite valuable, you know.'

'But Jake told me he's letting you have your sister's things. I was expecting to be able to get rid of all this clutter.'

She waved her arm in the direction of a number of objects which had been pushed towards the far wall. There was Ruth's embroidery frame on sturdy legs; the antique work basket which had belonged to her grandmother; a small, carved screen which she had fancied and bid on at an auction sale.

'I'm sure we can find a temporary home for those pieces,' Jenny agreed.

After all, if Jake wanted this woman to work here it was only fair that the room should be arranged for her convenience. Magda's face fell.

'Aren't you getting married soon then?'

'The marriage which was arranged will not now take place,' Jenny quoted, having seen that stilted piece of prose in an old novel.

'Oh, dear. So you'll be staying on for a bit, I suppose.'

'I haven't decided yet.'

Unless Jake actually asked her to go, there was no way that Jenny was prepared to go anywhere! She was about to leave the room when they heard a muffled thump, followed by a cry of pain. They rushed into the hall where they found Mary Gladstone sitting in a heap at the foot of the stairs.

'I do feel queer,' she quavered, tears pouring down her face. 'I stepped on something and slipped down the last couple of steps.'

A small toy dolls' pram, which Jenny recognised as belonging to Sheena's dolls' house, lay on the hall rug a few inches away.

'Mary, I'm so sorry. I've told her not to leave her toys lying about, but she never remembers. Do you think you can get up? Will I send for Dr Peters?'

Mary tried to struggle to her feet but fell back with a moan.

'It's my ankle. I think I've broken it.'

Jake arrived on the scene just at that moment and between them they managed to help Mary out to his car. Jake drove her to the hospital. Jenny would have liked to go, too, but she didn't want to leave Sheena to Magda Hall. Nor did she have the heart to scold the little girl for leaving her toy on the stairs because the expression on the little girl's wan face tugged at her heartstrings.

'Gladdie had an accident?'

'Yes, dear. Daddy's taken her to hospital.'

'My mummy had an accident, and the big men put her in a namalance and took her to hospital, and then she went to Heaven to see Jesus. Is Gladdie going to Heaven, too?'

Jenny hastened to reassure her.

'Goodness, no, darling. She'll soon be better and she'll be home again.'

'Oh, I thought Gladdie could go and say hello to Mummy.'

Jenny had a lump in her throat and was unable to reply.

'It's not broken,' Jake announced when he returned. 'Just a bad sprain. However, she has a slight concussion so they're keeping her under observation for a day or two. They think she probably fell backwards and hit her heard. She's worrying about our meals, of course. I suggested that Hoppy might step into the breech but that set her off properly. She swears Hoppy couldn't boil an egg and I mustn't let her loose in the kitchen. So that leaves you, Jenny Wren. Think you can handle it?'

'Actually, I'm quite a good cook,' Jenny assured him.

For the next few days Jenny served a series of delicious meals. Because she was determined not to leave Jake alone with Magda, who would doubtless have been better pleased to see her rival relegated to the status of servant, she and Sheena joined them in the dining-room. Sheena was thrilled to be eating with her daddy instead of being up in the day nursery.

'I'm a big girl now, aren't I, Daddy?'

She beamed at her father, who smiled back.

The only unhappy person at the table was Magda, who poked at her food with an expression of distaste on her lovely face while Jake praised Jenny's cooking to the skies, causing Magda to look even more sullen.

14

Mary Gladstone was soon home again, but she refused to rest comfortably in her suite of rooms as Jake suggested.

'I've only got a gammy leg. There's nothing wrong with my hands. I can sit in my kitchen just as well as I could upstairs, if someone brings my old footstool down for me. Jenny and I get on well together and I shan't mind sharing my kitchen for a while.'

So she sat in a sunny corner of the kitchen, happily peeling potatoes or shelling peas, while doling out advice to Jenny.

'It's easy to see you've a light hand with pastry, dear. Now let's see what you can make of a good steamed pudding. You know what they say about the way to a man's heart!'

Mary was now firmly on Jenny's side. As they worked together she regaled her assistant with countless tales of Jake's childhood, which Jenny greatly enjoyed. Also, Jake seemed more receptive to what Mary had to say since the shock of her accident, and had confided in her the story of Ruth's tragic ending.

'How can you possibly hold yourself responsible?' she demanded. 'Were you at the wheel of that car?'

'No,' he said miserably, 'but I knew she was in a state when she left here. I should have taken the keys from her, made her calm down first.'

'When your wife was worked up there was no reasoning with her. You know that as well as I do.'

Mary had lived in the house throughout their marriage and had known Ruth through and through.

'We are all responsible for our own actions, Mr Jake. Ruth herself was to blame if anybody was, but you know very well what they said at the inquest. It was ruled accidental death. No blame was attached to you, so why stay stuck in the past?'

Jake said nothing, but he looked thoughtful and Mary congratulated herself.

I put that rather well, if I do say so myself, she thought.

A week later, Mary Gladstone and Jenny were in the kitchen as usual, with Sheena playing happily at their feet, when they heard a heavy vehicle draw up outside.

'Look outside and see what that might be,' Mary said. 'My hands are all over flour and I want to get this cake in the oven before I stop for a cuppa.'

'It's a horse box! Do you suppose they've come to the wrong place?'

'Don't ask me, but Brooks will see to it.'

Brooks was the gardener. He now emerged from the stable block, evidently expecting the new arrivals. Jenny gave a squeak of surprise as a tall black gelding came down the ramp, led by a teenage boy in breeches and boots. What on earth was going on?

'It's a horse, Mary. I've got to go and

see this. Come on, Sheena, let's go and look.'

'Don't bang that door when you come back in,' Mary called after them, 'or you'll make my cake sink in the middle!'

The gelding was safely shut in a loose box by the time Jenny arrived. Brooks greeted her cheerfully.

'Hello, miss. What do you make of the master's new horse then?'

As they watched, the lad led another animal out of the horse box, this time a pretty mare, which Jenny judged to be about fifteen hands high.

'She's all pink, Auntie. Isn't she pretty?'

'She's called a strawberry roan, Sheena, and yes, she is lovely.'

The lad wasn't done yet, for stepping daintily down the ramp on polished little black hooves came a pretty dapple grey pony. Sheena clapped her hands.

'That one's just like my rocking horse, Auntie, only it doesn't have a red saddle. Is that pony for me?'

Having no idea what was going on, Jenny was glad to see Jake come striding across the yard. The lad stepped forward and tipped his cap.

'Hello, Johnson, all present and correct?' Jake asked.

'Yes, sir, and they had a smooth trip.'

'This is our new stable lad, Jenny. This is Miss Doyle, Johnson.'

'Pleased to meet you, miss.'

When the horses had been duly admired and the horse box had driven away, Jake and Jenny walked out to the paddock with Sheena hopping and skipping in front of them.

'They can stay indoors until they get over the excitement of the trip, but Johnson can turn them out here in the morning. He lives in the village with his mother so he doesn't need to stay here. He assures me he'll have no problem getting up at five o'clock in the morning and will be up here at six to muck out. He's been working in a factory ever since he left school and he's thrilled with the prospect of being in the open air again. We're to share him with Marsh at the riding school, so he'll find plenty to keep him busy.'

'It was such a surprise to see horses arriving. Why did you keep it such a secret?'

'The place hasn't been the same without them. Ruth was afraid of horses so there seemed to be no point keeping any, but now, Sheena seems to have taken to riding, thanks to you, so with her birthday coming up soon I've been on the lookout for a good, steady pony she can grow into. This one belonged to friends of mine. Tinkerbell, as they called her, was well-loved and ridden by each of their children in turn, but they're all too big for her now. She'll be a good starter pony for Sheena.'

'And the other horses?'

'The gelding is for me, the mare is for you.'

'For me!'

'Of course. You enjoy riding, don't you?'

'Yes, but what will happen to her

when I leave here?'

He put his hands on her shoulders and swung her round to face him.

'Never talk about leaving me again, Jenny. Tell me you're here to stay.'

He took her into his arms and kissed her passionately, releasing her reluctantly when she broke away from him and took a step backwards.

'What is it you're asking me, Jake?' she queried, breathless with hope.

'I don't have to spell it out, do I?' he said impatiently. 'I want you to marry me. What did you think I meant?'

'I didn't know for sure. But where does Magda fit into your plans?'

'Magda?'

He looked so puzzled that she had to laugh.

'She's my personal assistant, as you know. Will it bother you, having her working in the house when we're married? If it does, she can go back to the office.'

So Mary had been right, and Magda's hope of becoming engaged to

Jake had been no more than her wishful thinking. But there was one more thing to be cleared up.

'Wasn't there something between you at one time? I thought you were dating. You were together in the restaurant the night I went there with Seth.'

The night when Seth had proposed . . . She shuddered to remember how close she had come to marrying the wrong man.

'Oh, that. It was Magda's birthday, and the friends she was meant to be going out with had let her down. She asked me if I'd like to go out with her instead. I could hardly refuse. She's a valuable employee, after all.'

Poor Magda. Her image faded from Jenny's mind as Jake took her in his arms once more.

Later, they explained to Sheena that they'd be getting married. She did her best to understand, although Jenny suspected that, at not quite four years of age, she was really too young to take it in properly.

'Will you be my new mummy now?' she asked.

'I'll always be your own Auntie Jenny,' Jenny corrected her.

She would be the best mother she could be to her little niece, but she would never try to usurp Ruth's place in the child's heart. As the years went by she would keep Ruth's memory fresh by recounting stories of when Mummy was a little girl. As for the hurt that Ruth had inflicted on Jake and Jenny, that was all behind them now.

And so, a month later, the bells rang out at the little church in the village. Under the watchful eyes of all their family and friends, Jake vowed to love and honour Jenny until death parted them and in return she gladly pledged her love to him. Rhonda, newly engaged to Peter Steele, was bridesmaid, while little Sheena was a delightful flower girl.

As they drove off to begin their honeymoon they were waved away by all their guests who were lined up in the sunshine outside the Old Mill House. Both sets of parents were there, with Sheena hurling confetti. The staff was all there to wish them well — Mary Gladstone, Hoppy, Brooks and Johnson. Of Magda Hall there was no sign, nor had she sent them a wedding present.

Jenny looked back at the house with a heart full of joy.

'We'll be back soon,' she whispered as Jake took her hand in his.

They had both come through so much, but now they knew that it was their turn to love again.

THE END